Making love to Flora Graham wasn't something Josh was supposed to want to do....

It was supposed to be a means to an end, a close-your-eyes-and-think-of-revenge sort of situation!

The sexual chemistry was a bonus to be exploited, he told himself. She was vulnerable—seduction would be a walk in the park.

It was easy to exploit someone who didn't have a heart or feelings...but Flora could not keep hers disguised....

Kim Lawrence

A SEDUCTIVE REVENGE

TORONTO • NEW YORK • LONDON
AMSTERDAM • PARIS • SYDNEY • HAMBURG
STOCKHOLM • ATHENS • TOKYO • MILAN • MADRID
PRAGUE • WARSAW • BUDAPEST • AUCKLAND

ISBN 0-373-12171-7

A SEDUCTIVE REVENGE

First North American Publication 2001.

Copyright © 2000 by Kim Lawrence.

This edition published by arrangement with Harlequin Books S.A.

® and TM are trademarks of the publisher. Trademarks indicated with
® are registered in the United States Patent and Trademark Office, the
Canadian Trade Marks Office and in other countries.

Visit us at www.eHarlequin.com

Printed in U.S.A.

CHAPTER ONE

JOSH PRENTICE lifted his head and looked blankly at his agent. 'I've changed my mind.' He accompanied his bombshell with a languid smile that made Alec Jordan want to tear out what little hair he had left.

Josh wasn't just his most successful client, he was also his friend, and Alec knew he didn't have a languid bone in his well-built body. The older man regarded his friend's long-limbed, athletically built frame for a moment with wistful resentment.

'I've got a TV interview lined up for tomorrow night,' he explained for the third time with tight-lipped patience. 'The timing is perfect; your exhibition opens next week. The last interview you did after that art festival went down really well—apparently they love your cute French accent.' He gritted his teeth as his lavish flattery failed to make any impact on the younger man. 'I've already re-scheduled once because of Liam's birthday party.' He was unable to keep the sense of misuse from his voice. This was all the thanks he got for busting his butt rearranging things for an infuriatingly dedicated single parent!

'Thanks for the gift; Liam loved it.'

Alec sighed, seeing no hint of concession in those hard grey eyes, eyes which rarely softened these days for anyone other than his son. He allowed his thoughts to drift longingly in the direction of hungry artists starving in attics—how much more malleable, he mused wistfully, they must be than the likes of Josh, who, to add insult to injury didn't even have to rely on the healthy income from his

5

chosen career—it went against nature for an artist to also have business acumen.

'The flight to Paris is booked,' he persisted stubbornly.

'Then unbook it.' Josh remained unmoved as, with a deep, agonised groan, his agent slumped theatrically into the opposite chair, his head in his hands.

'Would it be too much to ask where you're going if it's not to Paris?' Alec enquired in a muffled voice. 'And don't give me any guff about artistic temperament because we both know you don't have any!'

Josh's lips quivered faintly at this hoarse accusation. 'Actually I'm not entirely sure yet...' He got to his feet and absent-mindedly tugged at the zip on his jacket, pulling the cloth taut across an impressive chest. He moved restlessly around the room before meeting Alec's interrogative stare.

His friend barely repressed the shudder that crawled up his spine at the detached, bone-chilling expression in those half-closed pale grey depths. Volcanic emotions, intense and fierce, were there simmering just below the surface. He hadn't seen Josh look like this since just after Bridie's death—during those bleak black days Josh had been totally consumed by a deep, smouldering rage and the only person brave or foolish enough to voluntarily expose himself to all that raw emotion had been his twin brother, Jake.

'It depends...I'm following someone.' Josh's firm, wide, unmistakably sensual lips compressed into a grim line as he contemplated the task ahead.

'Did you say f...following...?'

'A woman...' Josh tersely supplied, bringing to an abrupt halt his friend's incredulous stuttering.

'A woman!' A slow, relieved smile spread across Alec's face. At last—to hell with Paris, he decided magnanimously, this really was great news! 'About time too,' he boomed approvingly. It just wasn't natural, a man like Josh living like a monk. If he had half as many offers...! It wasn't as if anyone had expected the man to jump into bed with the first female who came along...but *three years* and he hadn't even looked... 'Why didn't you say? Who is she?'

'Flora Graham.'

Alec gasped, his florid complexion growing pale. 'You don't mean *the* Flora Graham. The daughter of...the one who...?'

Josh gave a wintry smile. 'The one who killed my wife?' He ignored Alec's agonised clucking sounds of denial, and wondered why everyone seemed so anxious to make excuses for David Graham—everybody but him, that was. 'The very same,' he confirmed calmly.

Alec, who'd half expected Josh to launch into a furious tirade at his own ill-advised protest, relaxed slightly. As unlikely pairings went, this one had him reeling.

It had taken Josh a long time to come to terms with the fact the young wife he'd adored had died during childbirth. The wounds had been dramatically reopened when it had come to light earlier that year that the much-respected doctor, Sir David Graham, who had been Bridie's obstetrician, was facing drug charges.

Actually the more lurid charges, which, it transpired, had been instigated by evidence supplied by a disgruntled employer who had tried to blackmail the surgeon into supplying her and her shady friends with drugs, had eventually been dropped. This hadn't stopped the media interest; the case had really caught their imagination.

The response from the legal community to Josh's accusations remained sympathetic but firm: their exhaustive enquiries hadn't revealed proof that any of his patients had ever suffered because of Sir David's problem. This attitude had exacerbated Josh's burning feelings of injustice and fuelled his desire for revenge.

Given Josh's feelings, Alec had been surprised at his lack of response when the details of the Graham court case had recently been plastered across every tabloid and broadsheet. Of course, if he'd fallen for the daughter that would explain...

'Stunning girl, of course.' The ice-cold blonde wasn't someone he'd personally like to spend a cosy evening with, but each to his own. Women like that could make him feel inadequate with one look; fortunately feelings of inadequacy were not something that kept Josh awake nights. 'Very...very...blonde,' he managed lamely. 'Had no idea you even knew her! How did you meet?'

'We haven't—yet—that's why I'm following her,' Josh explained patiently.

Alec suddenly had a cold premonition in the pit of his belly. 'What are you going to do when you do meet her?' he enquired, suddenly fearful of the reply.

On several occasions Flora Graham had had the opportunity to publicly condemn her father but she'd steadfastly refused to do so. Josh could still hear the beautifully modulated voice, which fairly shrieked of privilege, defending her parent as she'd responded with clinical precision to her public interrogations; his smile deepened. The father might be out of circulation, having chosen to spend time in a rehabilitation centre rather than serve an equally derisory prison sentence, but the daughter was still around, and, according to his sources, about to leave town.

The drug-dealing doctor whom weeks before the tabloids had hated had suddenly, with the typical fickleness of the popular press, become a pitiful figure, a victim, who'd harmed nobody but himself and had actually acted honourably when it had counted. It was the final straw!

Normally Josh was extremely tolerant of weaknesses—at least in others—but this case was a notable exception.

The heavy eyelids drooped over his silver-shot eyes. 'The details are a bit hazy as yet, but making her *deeply* unhappy is the general theme I'm aiming for.' And if that meant sleeping with her, so be it.

It was over an hour after she'd left the motorway before Flora knew for sure she was being followed—as scummy rats went, this one was quite efficient. She glared at the image of the red coupé in the rear-view mirror and something inside snapped. The voracious media had made her life a misery for the past months…wasn't it enough that she was reduced to sneaking out of town like some sort of criminal?

Enough was definitely enough! She braked sharply as the lay-by, half hidden from the winding road by a copse of trees, came into view. She wasn't exactly overcome with surprise when the flashy red car, its wheels sending up a flurry of loose chippings, pulled in a little way in front of her.

Knuckles white on the steering wheel, she took a deep, steadying breath—it was about time she stopped acting like a victim and gave them a taste of their own medicine! To hell with reticence and diplomacy! Her heels beat out a sharp tattoo as she marched purposefully towards the car. She made no attempt to confront the driver, instead she knelt beside the rear wheel and, after a moment's adjustment, heard the satisfying hiss of air escaping from the tyre.

Revenge might just have something to recommend it, she decided with a smile. She was rubbing her hands together in satisfaction when the driver of the vehicle emerged.

'What the hell?'

She recognised the thickset figure as one of the most persistent amongst the pack of journalists who had camped on her doorstep for days on end. It was the sheer incredulity in his face as he stared at the slowly deflating tyre that made Flora laugh, though in retrospect she swiftly acknowledged that the laugh probably hadn't been such a good idea—he was a big man and in a very ugly mood.

Why hadn't she sensibly driven to the nearest police station to get rid of her unwanted companion? What she'd been too angry to take into account earlier now struck her with sickening force—this was a very lonely road in a fairly remote area. At that moment, as if to emphasise the sinister implications of the situation, the wind gave an extra strong gust causing the tall trees to whisper menacingly overhead. She could almost hear them snigger, Talk yourself out of this one, Flora.

'You little cow!' The driver seemed to have recovered from his catatonic state and he was walking slowly towards her.

Flora found her feet stupidly wouldn't move from the spot as the big bulky figure approached her.

'That's criminal damage.' The words sounded so much like those of a sulky, thwarted child that Flora's moment of panic vanished.

'So is going through someone's dustbins,' she corrected with some feeling, 'and if it isn't it should be! Take your hands off me!' She gasped in outrage as the big ape wrapped one beefy paw around her forearm; his grip didn't loosen when she pulled angrily away and the stylish felt cloche she wore on her head slipped over one eye.

He wasn't going to hurt her, but it gave Tom Channing a sharp thrill of satisfaction to know that under that haughty façade Miss Ice Cool might be scared. All those weeks under the cruel light of public scrutiny and her composure hadn't cracked—not even once! People in her situation were meant to feel out of control and vulnerable but somehow this stuck-up little cow managed to act as if she didn't notice the flashing bulbs wherever she went—it just wasn't natural!

To add insult to injury even her friends had turned out to be untraditionally tight-lipped and stubbornly loyal. They'd closed ranks and to a man had refused to dish the dirt! She'd grown to represent everything about her class he detested. In a brief moment of rare honesty he realised that the fact probably had a lot to do with his reluctance to let the story die a natural death even though public interest in the scandal had waned. This was a crusade of a deeply personal nature now.

'What you going to do about it if I don't, Miss Graham?' he taunted, revelling in the heady feeling of being in control.

'Is there a problem here?'

The man holding her turned around with a frustrated snarl on his face. If Flora had been looking at her stalker she might have appreciated the comical speed with which his combative glare became a weak, conciliatory grin. Only Flora wasn't looking at him, she was looking—well, actually, to be strictly honest, which she tried at all times to be—she was staring. Staring at the owner of the rich deep voice, riveting long-lashed slate-grey eyes, and sinfully sexy mouth.

There was quite a lot of him to stare at—he must be six-four or six-five, she estimated, paying silent, stunned homage to the sheer perfection of this athletically built specimen. His shoulders wouldn't have looked out of place competitively employed in an Olympic swimming pool and she could almost see those sprinter's legs eating up the track…everything in between looked just about perfect too. He broadcast raw sex appeal on a frequency every female with a pulse would have picked up at fifty yards. On second thoughts, maybe there wasn't a safe distance from this man!

Flora let out a tiny grunt of shock as her breath escaped gustily past her slightly parted lips. She wasn't the sort of girl who made a habit of mentally undressing men, especially a married man as this one obviously was—the cute little boy beside him was too much of a carbon copy not to be his son, and then there was the little matter of the wide gold band on his left hand!

Fantasising about married men was not a pastime Flora indulged in—in fact, considering that she'd been very publicly dumped by her ever-loving fiancé, she ought not to be capable of anything so frivolous! I'm probably just a disgustingly shallow person, she concluded, reviewing her worryingly resilient heart critically.

'Just a little misunderstanding…' Her stalker saw the direction of those narrowed grey eyes and his hand dropped self-consciously away from Flora's arm. Although the tall guy was smiling—the curve of his mouth didn't soften those chiselled features or spookily pale eyes an iota—and he had a grubby-faced toddler glued to his leg, didn't lessen the fact he looked a dangerously tough customer. There was something vaguely familiar about him too…

Flora fastidiously gave a disbelieving snort and flicked her fingers against the invisibly soiled area of her sleeve. Angrily she straightened the drunken angle of her hat. Next he'd be saying he'd *accidentally* followed her.

She bit back the scathing retort on the tip of her tongue—once you started acting spontaneously it was hard to stop—and summoned a tight smile. More detailed explanations would inevitably mean the handsome stranger getting a potted version of the whole sordid saga. It struck her as perverse that she suddenly felt so squeamish about such a small-scale exposure after what she'd managed to survive.

'I might take issue with the "little"—' her deep blue eyes swept scornfully over the persistent journalist's face '—but I'm fine, thank you.'

Happily the stranger, despite his unconvinced expression, didn't take issue with her lie. He turned to the hack who was nudging his flat tyre with the tip of his boot.

'Flat...?'

The journalist jerked his head in response and shot Flora a murderous glare. 'I'm not carrying a spare,' he realised with a groan.

'Bad luck,' Josh responded blandly. His natural inclination was to assume that anyone giving Flora Graham and her family a hard time couldn't be all bad, but in this case he was prepared to modify his views; he had disliked the guy on sight—a real sleaze bag!

As he turned his head he caught Flora's violet-blue eyes and winked. Dazed by the blast of charm aimed in her direction, she helplessly grinned back at him.

Josh froze and didn't catch what his son said in his urgent infant treble. He was mega unprepared for the transformation from cold goddess to warm, vibrant woman. The faint wrinkles around her suddenly warm blue eyes and the conspiratorial crooked little smile were bad enough, but it was the slight indentation in her porcelain-smooth left cheek that was the real clincher. A dimple! He found he really objected deeply to the fact Flora Graham had a dimple; neither the glimpses he'd had of her outside the courtroom or the image of her impassively enduring television interviews had even suggested such a thing.

Flora was accustomed, even before her face had been plastered across the front page of several tabloids, to men looking at her—this definitely wasn't *that* sort of look! Which was a relief because the pleasure of being admired for something as superficial as the neat arrangement of her regular, and to her mind somewhat insipidly pretty, features, or the tautness of her slim, athletic figure had palled years ago. She knew to her cost that none of these would-be admirers gave a damn about what sort of woman lay beneath the attractive window-dressing.

Whilst she didn't mind this hunk not being bowled over by her beauty—a small ironic grimace flickered across her features at the notion—something about that stare did trouble her. A small frown puckered her smooth forehead, and distant warning bells sounded in her head. She closed her mouth and surreptitiously explored with her tongue the possibility she had some unsightly remnant of her lunch stuck in her teeth.

'My phone's not working, mate. Have you...?' The journalist tentatively approached the silent couple.

'No reception up here...probably the mountains,' Josh elaborated, gesturing with a strong, shapely hand towards the breathtaking but forbidding scenery. 'I seem to recall there was a garage about half a mile back...'

Flora had followed the direction of his hand, registering automatically the strong, shapely part, and she found herself comparing this stranger with the landscape—more rugged and dangerous than pastoral. She dismissed the instinct of moments before that had suggested something wasn't quite right; after all, if her instinct was so reliable what had she been doing engaged to Paul, the ratbag?

'I don't suppose there's any chance of a lift...?' The sardonic quirk of one dark brow brought a rush of colour; it was clearly visible even through Tom Channing's care-

fully nurtured designer stubble, which was meant to under-
line, along with the single gold ring in one ear and the
scuffed shoes, his hard-man street credibility. It narked him
no end that this big guy had buckets of the stuff and he
didn't even try. 'That's a no, I take it,' he concluded bitterly.

Flora had to bite her lip to prevent herself from grinning
as she watched the burly figure flounce off to his car mut-
tering—carefully not loud enough for her companion to
hear—under his breath.

'I think you hurt his feelings.' It was hard not to gloat
so she gave up trying; she was due a bit of gloating.
'You're not meant to drive with a flat tyre, are you?' she
added innocently as the red car bumpily drew away.

'No.'

'I thought not.' Flora gave a contented sigh.

'Daddy!'

This time the urgent tugging at his trouser leg got Josh's
attention.

'What is it, champ?'

'I think I'm going to be sick!'

Stunned at the speed with which this prediction came
true, Flora stared in fascinated horror down at the unpleasant mess congealing over her pale biscuit trousers and favourite soft, handmade loafers.

'I feel better now.' Liam sighed and looked up happily
at his father.

Josh smiled back, silently congratulating his son on his
unerring aim. He produced a tissue to wipe the toddler's
mouth and glanced surreptitiously towards the tall, wil-
lowy blonde, fully expecting her to be close to a state of
complete collapse by now.

In his experience women like her, the sort who never
ventured out into public without the full works—make-up,
smooth, impossibly shiny hair and the season's latest in

designer gear—had a problem with the less picturesque aspects of life. And a kid throwing up fell safely into that category! He had to concede that a kid throwing up so comprehensively over you would have been enough to throw even those women of his acquaintance *not* totally preoccupied with their own appearance.

'I'm glad you feel better. I must say I feel rather yucky!'

Josh gave a disgruntled frown. There was a rueful twinkle in Flora's eyes as she smiled sweetly at his son. Damn woman, he didn't much like having to throw his script out of the window.

'You smell,' Liam told her frankly.

Flora's nose wrinkled. 'I'd noticed that too,' she admitted drily.

'You need a bath. Doesn't she, Daddy?'

Josh gave a noncommittal grunt. He suddenly had a very clear picture in his head of water sliding over satiny skin, gliding slowly down the slim, supple line of a naked female back. Her buttocks would be high and tight, you could tell by the way—his head snapped up so sharply a jarring pain shot all the way down his stiff spine. *Hell!* What a time for his libido to come out of hibernation.

But it wasn't the content of his lustful thoughts that made his guts tighten with a guilty repugnance, it was the person responsible for inciting those lustful thoughts. The whole situation suggested to him that someone up there had one twisted sense of humour!

A warm bubble of humour escaped from Flora's throat. 'Or, failing that, a change of clothes,' she agreed solemnly. She shifted her weight and her shoes squelched rather disgustingly. 'Also I have a pack of Wet Wipes—a *large* pack.'

Josh scooped his talkative son up into his arms. 'I'm sorry about this, Miss...?'

He fixed on his best guileless-stroke-helpless smile. It was the one that had females of all ages stampeding to help him with his son and he wasn't above using it if the occasion warranted it. He'd gone past the period when he'd needed to prove he could cope alone; now he wasn't so averse to making life easier.

She sighed—blessed anonymity! 'Flora,' she supplied, meeting the tall stranger's eyes and feeling inexplicably shy.

'I'm Josh, Josh Prentice, and this is Liam who, as you have probably gathered, isn't the world's best traveller.' He held out his hand towards her. 'You must bill me for the clothes.'

Flora grimaced and wriggled her less-than-clean fingers a safe distance away. 'For your safety I think we should pass on that one. As for the clothes, I'd say we're even.' She gave a sigh as she contemplated the sticky situation he'd rescued her from. 'When I'm around creeps like that I *really* wish I were a man. Don't get me wrong,' she added swiftly, just in case he imagined she was a bit of a wimp, 'I can handle men like that. You just have to be more subtle,' she explained to her rather startled-looking audience.

She'd learnt early on that men could be intimidated by the combination of cut-glass beauty and brains, and sometimes that combination allied with a cutting tongue was the only weapon she had or needed—*usually*.

Friends who knew she was a bit of a softy thought it a hoot when they saw her turn on the 'deep freeze' but this ability had come in really handy recently when, traumatised deeply by the unkind public scrutiny, not to mention the fact the father she'd worshipped all her life had been exposed as a drug addict—life really was stranger than fiction—she'd retreated behind a mask of aloof disdain.

Firmly repressing the troublesome urge to continue to stare up at him, she transferred her gaze to a far less complex pair of grey eyes fringed by lashes just as preposterously long as in the older version.

'Ever tried ginger biscuits for travel sickness, Liam?' The kiddy looked predictably interested at the mention of food. 'They work for me. In fact, I've probably got some in my car. They might help settle his tummy…?' she suggested tentatively to Josh.

Some people donned dark glasses and wig to escape notice; it seemed Miss Graham donned a different personality—she was behaving like a girl guide! Still, he'd be around when she showed her true colours. At that moment she swept off her hat and he saw the disguise didn't stop there!

The long, waist-length shimmering mane of silvery blonde hair was gone, replaced by a short feathery cap that followed the elegant shape of her skull. The style might lack the impact of long, swishy blonde tresses, but the gamin cut did make her eyes look bigger, her patrician features more delicate, and emphasised the long, graceful curve of her neck. Let's face it, with bones like hers the girl could shave off her hair and still look stunning!

Flora lifted her hand to her head and felt an instant's surprise when her fingers made contact with the short, wavy strands. Just contemplating how much Paul would dislike it made her feel cheerful about her rebellious gesture. Her ex-fiancé had once confided, in one of his rare moments of honesty—did *all* politicians lie?—that he thought women with short hair were unfeminine, and probably a bit confused about their sexuality.

Now she could see what had been blindingly obvious all the time: he *hadn't* been joking; this comment was typical of the man; Paul was a first-class narrow-minded bigot! And I was going to bear his children! She shook her head slightly as she considered her criminal lack of judgement when it came to men.

'Have you got far to travel, Flora?' Josh hoped not—another half-hour in the car with Liam and he might go completely gaga. It had afforded him dark amusement when the car following Flora had been so busy trying not to be noticed that the driver had failed to suspect that someone else had the same quarry in mind.

It had made his own task easier, but not that easy. Liam's low boredom threshold and dislike of car journeys were two things he foolishly hadn't taken into account when he'd set out to follow Flora Graham out of town.

Flora got a nice warm glow as she watched Josh jiggle the little boy from one narrow hip to the other, absently kissing the toddler's nose as he did so. He seemed not to notice that the child's grubby hands had comprehensively mussed up his glossy dark hair. After Paul, who had been almost pathological about neatness—and still was, no doubt—it was quite a contrast.

She was off men permanently, because they were more trouble than they were worth, but she couldn't help thinking... Her eyes moved covetously over his long, lean frame. This other woman's husband was so spectacularly delicious, and great with the kiddy. Nice, incredible-looking and oozing daddy appeal—why don't I ever meet men like that? she wondered indignantly.

He wouldn't have to be *that* good-looking. In fact, perhaps it might be better if he wasn't, she concluded wryly, then hungry single women wouldn't be lusting after him when my back was turned. Women like me! A guilty flush mounted her cheeks and she replied a little stiltedly.

'A friend has a holiday cottage not far from here.' She named the little village. 'Do you know it?' The stranger inclined his dark head in confirmation and she blithely chattered on. After being forced by circumstances to be discreet to the point of dumbness in front of strangers, it was something of a relief to talk normally—well, not totally normally, she felt impelled to admit.

The man was just too damned gorgeous to be able to do anything in front of him totally unselfconsciously. She was ruefully aware that a very unsolicitor-like girly giggle—the one she had to repress if she didn't want him to think she was a brainless bimbo—was only a heartbeat away.

'That is not far; but far enough to make a change of clothes a must.' Her nose twitched in an attempt to avoid the sour smell emanating from her person. 'I need to change. I don't suppose you could...?' She stopped mid-request with a self-conscious grimace. 'No, of course you couldn't...'

'It has been known for me to answer for myself.'

She grinned. 'I bet it has,' she responded, examining his determined angular jawline; doting dad or not, he looked like the opinionated type to her. 'Actually I was hoping you could act as lookout for me whilst I change. It could be a bit embarrassing if I'm stripped off down to my undies when some family pulls up complete with picnic basket...'

'I'd have thought you'd have been more concerned about lone males, but I was forgetting you can handle men...*subtly*...'

Was there a strand of mockery in his deep voice? Flora felt vaguely uneasy as she watched him put down the child and brush his hands against his strong, muscular thighs. There was nothing remotely sexual about the gesture—the sex, she told herself sternly, was all in her own mind—but that didn't stop her body temperature hiking up several notches. This entire weird overreaction was probably all part of the winding-down process. After the last few months that wasn't going to be an overnight thing.

'Realistically I don't suppose there's much chance of *anyone* coming along here.' A cooling-off period was urgently required, so she allowed her eyes to drift around the rather bleak landscape before coming to rest once more on his face.

'I did.'

'It's probably lucky for me you did.' She didn't think she'd been in any actual physical danger from the journalist, just the sort of unpleasant scene which she would much rather avoid.

Lamb to the slaughter, Josh marvelled as she looked up at him oozing trust and lack of suspicion. He ought to be feeling pretty pleased with how things were going, but somehow her trusting disposition was irritating the hell out of him.

'I wouldn't want you to risk indecent exposure charges.'

Flora's eyes widened, a hard laugh was wrenched from her throat. 'Wouldn't they have loved that!'

'Pardon…?'

Flora gathered her wits. Small wonder he was looking at her blankly. 'It's a long story.'

'And none of my business.'

Flora flushed, aware that at the first hint of the conversation growing remotely personal she had automatically reverted to cool disdain. 'Actually it's not something I want to talk about.'

'And I'm a stranger.'

'But a very kind one,' she told him warmly. She couldn't understand why his handsome face hardened.

'And if I wasn't—if I was a dangerous, marauding lone

male with evil intentions—you could deal with me... right?'

Flora laughed a little uneasily and tried not to notice the way her stomach lurched when she visualised how it might feel if that horrifying scenario were true.

'But you're not alone, you're with Liam...you're a *father*.'

'And being a father places me above suspicion...and temptation?' He silently reviewed the lists of world-class baddies who'd been doting dads, but resisted the impulse to point out the obvious flaws in her argument. 'I must admit I've never quite looked at it in that way before. I'm overcome by the confidence you place in me.'

Flora didn't think he sounded overcome, just irked. Perhaps even happily married men preferred to think they could still be considered dangerous.

'There's nothing wrong with being domesticated,' she told him kindly. Actually she didn't think half a dozen kids could make this particular specimen appear domesticated. She was a sensible, mature woman—*mostly*—with her feet firmly on the ground, and even her stomach showed a dangerous tendency to go all squidgy when she looked into those hooded silvery eyes.

'And it's nothing to do with paternity as such.' She frowned earnestly. 'Don't you ever just get a gut feeling with some people that you can trust them?' She closed her mouth with an audible snap...where the hell did that come from?

Squirming with humiliation, she gazed at the dark colour that stained the sharp, high angle of his achingly perfect cheekbones. Now I've embarrassed him—small wonder! You don't go around telling total strangers you have gut feelings about them—gut feelings suggest a degree of intimacy! He probably thinks I'm making a pass at him or something. It was true about the gut feeling, though...

Josh broke the awkward silence. 'Liam's been cramped in the car all morning; he needs a chance to stretch his legs.' To her relief he was acting as if she'd said nothing out of the ordinary. 'If you want to change I'll keep an eye out for coach parties.'

'Well, if you're...thanks...'

Josh kept one eye on his son who was building a tower with the stray rocks he'd gathered and the other on the wing mirror of his four-wheel drive, which kept him up to date with the state of play of Flora's contortions in the back seat of her small car.

Now wasn't the time to be worrying about the general scumminess of such behaviour. He couldn't afford the luxury of scruples if he was going to make Graham pay. He was going to hit him where it hurt and Graham's Achilles' heel was his daughter—he adored her. The moment Josh had seen the interview of the two of them together he'd known that this was the way to make him pay. As for the girl, she hadn't even been willing to admit her father had done anything wrong. As always when he needed reminding of why he was doing this, he brought the picture of Bridie's sweet, laughing face to mind—or he would have if what was going on in the car hadn't distracted him.

Any travellers seeking a respite from their journey at that moment wouldn't have been treated to the sight of Flora's underwear. She wasn't wearing any—at least not from the waist up, which was the bit he could see. Her breasts were fairly small, pointed and high. They bounced energetically as she stretched upwards, pulling a thin cashmere polo shirt over her head. With a muffled curse of self-disgust Josh tore his eyes away.

Who was he kidding? This had nothing to do with revenge; it was pure voyeurism. That was bad, but not so bad if all he'd wanted to do was look!

He heard the sound of her feet on the rough ground but didn't turn around. He watched as Liam carefully selected a stick and knocked down the tower of rocks he'd so lovingly constructed.

'I worry about his aggressive instincts sometimes.'

'I wouldn't, it's perfectly normal,' Flora comforted. She smiled as the youngster laughed out loud before he started to rebuild his destroyed creation. 'I'm sure you did the same.'

'No, my brother Jake built them and I knocked them down, then he knocked me down. These days people pay him a lot of money to build things and nobody knocks them down.'

'He's a builder?'

'No, an architect.'

'And what do you do?' She bit her lip. 'You don't have to answer that—once I get into interrogation mode there's no stopping me,' she babbled in embarrassment.

'So what does that make you?' He responded to Liam's pouting plea by producing a sweet from his pocket. 'Only one,' he warned before handing it over. 'A police woman...?' he suggested, straightening up from his crouched pose and brushing his hands against the seat of his well-worn denims.

'No, a solicitor.'

'Pity...'

She looked enquiringly at him.

'I've always had a soft spot for a girl in uniform.'

His smile and the way her heart started to beat wildly filled her with panic. 'Is Liam an only child?' A swift diplomatic change of subject was urgently required.

Josh didn't reply straight away; when he did his grey

eyes held a shadowy expression that disturbed her. Was she imagining the tenseness in his greyhound-lean body?

'Yes, he is.'

He was young, maybe thirty; he and his wife could produce a lot more children all as enchanting as Liam. Flora, who had never been aware of any strong maternal instincts, felt a surge of envy and a deepening sense of dissatisfaction with where her life was going.

'So am I.'

A nerve throbbed in Josh's lean cheek. 'That must make you all the more precious to your parents.' His eyes were curiously intent on her face.

'Father; my mum died five years ago.'

He touched her hand—hardly even a touch, more a brushing of her skin; the gesture seemed unpremeditated. Flora didn't move. She continued to stare at the busy, happy child, aware all the time of an invisible web of nerve-endings she hadn't even known existed surge to zinging life all over her body. Her skin felt so alive it hurt—pleasure bordering on pain. She found herself completely unprepared for this raw, sensual awakening.

The symptoms dissipated but didn't vanish when his hand fell away. Way out of proportion or what? Her puffily exhaled breath turned white in the chill of the lengthening autumnal afternoon.

'I better be going,' she said, swallowing hard and stirring the loose ground with the toe of her casual flat shoe.

Josh noticed the replacement was just as expensive and exclusive as the one she'd worn earlier. Daddy's indulged little girl...it didn't work; his rage only responded sluggishly to the prod.

'Thank you,' she began with a frank, open smile. 'For everything.' If she drew this out much longer he was going to realise she felt reluctant to leave...it was quite absurd.

His mental preparations hadn't prepared him for this. Making love to Flora Graham wasn't something he was supposed to *want* to do. It was supposed to be a means to an end, a 'close your eyes and think of revenge' sort of situation! It was easy to exploit someone who obviously didn't have a heart or feelings. This stupid woman didn't only have them, she didn't even keep them decently disguised.

This could be so easy; she'd been shaking like a nervous thoroughbred when he'd touched her. The sexual chemistry was a bonus to be exploited, he told himself. She trusted him, her father had just been publicly disgraced, her fiancé had dumped her, she was vulnerable, seduction would be a walk in the park. Telling her the truth would be a pleasure. All he had to do was go gently...

Nobody had ever accused Josh Prentice of taking the easy option!

He had a mouth which knew exactly what to do to reduce his victim to a state of helpless and humiliating cooperation. The searing onslaught of his clever tongue and lips went beyond the physical.

Flora staggered backwards when the pressure ceased and the big hands that had held her face fell away. She continued to stagger until her spine made contact with a convenient tree; the rough surface abraded her back through the thin, hooded top she now wore over a polo shirt. Breathing shallow and fast, she reached behind her to clutch the comforting solidity of the bark in what had become an almost surreal world.

'Why,' she asked in a voice which hovered on the brink of tremulous, 'did you do that?' Good, her voice was beginning to get back to normal.

Kissing her didn't seem to have put him in a mellow frame of mind, although at the time it had seemed to her he'd been enjoying himself! She was humiliatingly aware of the ache in her taut, peaking breasts.

'I had to see for myself if you were as stupid as you look!' he snapped cuttingly.

The outrage on his voice made her blink. 'And am I?' she enquired in a dazed voice.

'With bells on, woman!' he raged. 'Don't you have *any* sense of self-preservation? I could have been anyone and you come out with all that airy-fairy crap about trust. *Trust!*' He choked. 'I could be Jack the bloody Ripper for all you know and all you can do is look at me as if I...' With a snort of disgust he broke off. 'Just because you like the way someone looks, it doesn't make them all the things you want them to be.' He was warning her, you couldn't get fairer than that. Or more stupid, a quiet inner voice sighed.

Two spots of dark colour stained the soft contours of her pale cheeks. Was I really *that* obvious?

'What makes you think,' she snapped with cold precision, 'that I like the way you look?'

He threw back his head and laughed; it was a bitter sound. 'Like you don't like the way I kiss?' One dark, strongly delineated brow shot satirically upwards. 'I noticed the way you *hated* that.'

Flora's face was burning with mortification at his soft, derisive jibe—so what if she might have co-operated for a split second? 'Most men wouldn't be complaining,' she said, glaring up at his hatefully handsome face. She bit her lips as she realised it was too late now to dispute the claim she'd in any way enjoyed being kissed by him. 'But then you only kissed me out of the goodness of your heart to show me how foolishly trusting I was being...teach me a lesson...'

There was more than a grain of truth in her sarcastic

jibe, but it wasn't the entire story. He ran an exasperated hand through his dark hair. 'I kissed you,' he hissed in a driven voice, 'because I wanted to.' Abruptly he turned away from his contemplation of the trees; his deep-set eyes burned into her.

The air whooshed out of her lungs. 'Oh!' Her eyes searched his face. Given the circumstances, it wasn't very flattering that he looked as if he were trying to digest something particularly bitter and unappetising.

She smiled distractedly at Liam, who opened his grubby little hand to offer her a smooth black stone. 'Black,' he explained patiently.

'It's his favourite colour,' his father elaborated tersely.

'Lovely, Liam.' She smiled, pocketing the gift. 'Thank you.'

She stiffened. Am I slow or what? How could I have forgotten a *minor* detail like the ring on his finger, especially when the physical proof of the wretched man's unavailability is playing around my feet? What is wrong with me? I've had better kisses than that and not ended up with mush for a brain. It was a mistake to think about the kiss…stop hyperventilating, Flora.

'Does your wife know you go around doing things because you *want* to?' she enquired with icy derision. Her cold pose slipped. 'I think you're the most disgusting man I've ever met!' she told him in a quivering voice.

The pain that swept across his face made Flora's voice fade dramatically away. It occurred to her that she could never despise him half as much as he did himself.

'My wife's dead.' His voice sounded the same way.

Flora didn't know how to respond and he didn't appear to expect her to.

'I haven't wanted to kiss a woman since…' The harsh explanation emerged involuntarily.

Flora closed her eyes against a sudden rush of hot, emotional tears and wished he hadn't told her that. She'd come out here to regain a bit of inner peace, not get mixed up with some moody, brooding type who was way too good-looking. He'd got a kid, and—hell!—even more unresolved angst than she had. He was the one that introduced the subject of self-preservation.

Flora's heart ached as she watched them go, but she made no move to prevent them. She had troubles enough of her own without courting the extra ones a man like this one represented.

CHAPTER TWO

'NIA didn't say you were coming.' Megan Jones handed her husband, who was sitting with his heavily plastered leg propped up on a footstool, a fresh cup of tea.

'No.' Josh helped himself to another slice of his brother's mother-in-law's excellent *bara brith*. 'It was a spur of the moment thing.'

Megan Jones nodded understandingly. 'You need a break; Nia says you work far too hard.'

'Does she…?' He suspected his sister-in-law said far too much entirely. The next statement from one of her brothers confirmed this suspicion.

The kitchen door swung open. 'Nia says you need a woman, Josh. Like the haircut,' he added. 'Not so girly, makes you look nearly respectable.'

'Geraint!' his mother exclaimed, slapping her large, burly son's hand as he filched a slice of cake and crammed it whole into his mouth. 'Josh *is* respectable!' She flashed Josh a worried look and was relieved to see her guest didn't look offended by the slur. 'And look what your boots are doing to my nice clean floor,' she scolded her big son half-heartedly.

'I'll be back from Betws before milking, Mam,' her grinning son promised unrepentantly. He winked at Josh and ruffled Liam's hair before he departed just as speedily as he'd arrived.

'Now there's someone who is *definitely* working too hard,' his mother announced with a worried frown.

'I've told you I'd take on another man if we could afford

it.' Geraint's father gritted his teeth in frustration. 'You'd think with five sons there'd be more than one around the place when you need them,' he complained.

'Yes, well, I'm sure Josh doesn't want to hear us grumbling,' Megan said, pinning a bright smile on her face.

No wonder Megan was looking strained; Josh suspected that energetic Huw Jones was not an easy patient.

'I don't suppose there's ever a good time to break your leg, Huw…?'

'But some times are worse than others,' Huw rumbled, 'you've got it right there, boy.'

'Where are you staying, Josh?'

'I was hoping you could recommend somewhere nearby.'

'You couldn't do much better than The Panton,' Huw responded. 'Though it'll cost you an arm and leg.'

'The Panton, Huw, really!' Megan chided indignantly. 'Josh and Liam will stay with us, of course. Just like they always do. I miss having a child about the place.' She smiled fondly at Liam.

Since Jake had married Nia, Josh, a keen climber, had joined his brother here at Bryn Goleu for several weekend climbing expeditions in the rugged Snowdonian mountains. Megan Jones's hospitality was as warm as her smile.

'I think you've got your hands full without extra guests right now, Megan. We wouldn't dream of imposing.' Josh saw his hostess looked inclined to press the issue and a workable compromise occurred to him. 'I will stay, on one condition: you let me work for our board. I don't know a cow from a sheep,' he warned them with a grin, 'but I'm a willing pair of hands.' He held out his hands to demonstrate their willingness.

'We wouldn't dream…' Megan began politely.

Huw put aside his newspaper. 'What do you mean,

woman? Of course we'd dream. Beside, a bit of honest sweat'll do the boy a world of good, build up a bit of muscle.'

Josh took the scornful inference he was some sort of seven-stone weakling in his stride.

'If you let him talk much longer, Josh, he'll convince you you ought to be paying him for the privilege of letting you break your back!' Megan threw her husband a withering glance, but Josh could see she felt just as relieved as the reluctant invalid. Their gratitude made him feel guilty because his offer of help wasn't entirely altruistic. He hadn't been able to believe his luck when Flora had named the village she was staying in as one a mere mile from the Jones farm—it suited him very well to stay for a while at Bryn Goleu.

Flora's walking boots had never actually seen a puddle before; the country experience was proving a baptism by fire for her and them both. The boots seemed to be coping better with water than she had with the mouse in the house last night. Fortunately the village store stocked mousetraps, but Flora wasn't sure which horrified her most: the idea of coming face to face with a live mouse or a dead one.

She consulted the map in her pocket; if she was reading it correctly this footpath would cut her return journey by half. It seemed to go directly through a farmyard. Right on cue a farmyard came into view around the bend. She'd heard tales that suggested all farmers weren't exactly welcoming to ramblers; she hoped these natives, if she came across any, were friendly. Still, she reasoned, they couldn't possibly be as bad as tabloid journalists.

She did see one—it was hard to miss him—a large, shirtless specimen wheeling a barrow piled with fencing posts out of one of the stone outbuildings. His back was turned to her; it suggested he would make short work of driving those heavy wooden posts into the ground. She tried not to stare too obviously at the sculpted power of those rippling, tightly packed muscles; she had limited success.

She cleared her throat to let him know she was there. 'Good morning,' she called out politely. The figure turned slowly.

'*Bore da*, Flora.' Josh exhausted the limit of his Welsh.

She must have walked into the shop and bought it all up, he decided, giving her a quick once-over from her sunlit hair to her shiny new boots. All the stylish, squeaky new clothes were top-of-the-range mountain gear which showed off her lovely long length of leg and neat, incredibly small waist. A light crop of freckles had emerged across the bridge of her nose and her cheeks were healthily flushed, whether from exertion or from the shock of seeing him he wasn't quite sure...but he had his suspicions.

'*You!*' Flora, who had forgotten to breathe for several stupefied moments, took a deep noisy gulp to compensate.

'It's enough to make a man believe in coincidence,' he drawled, lifting a hand to shade his eyes from the sun.

She nodded in a dazed sort of way. Looking at her with a clear-eyed sardonic grey gaze, he was displaying none of the awkwardness she, because of the way they'd parted, felt—he didn't even seem surprised to see her. Willing her eyes not to make any detours over his naked torso, she kept them firmly trained on his face.

'Or fate.' Now why, she wondered with a silent groan, did I say that?

'And do you?' he enquired, unexpectedly expanding on the theme. 'Believe in fate?' He speared a pitchfork into the ground and leaned on it to casually watch her. Flora found the unblinking scrutiny uncomfortable.

Her curiosity reached boiling point and she succumbed to growing temptation and risked a quick, surreptitious peek at his leanly muscled chest and flat belly. Her stomach muscles did uncomfortable and worrying things. The earthy image hadn't done anything to soothe her jangled nerves or hot cheeks.

It was the little details like the line of hair that disappeared like a directional arrow beneath the waistband of the worn blue jeans he wore that got her especially hot under the collar. She wondered what he'd make of it if she picked up the discarded plaid shirt she'd spotted and begged him to put it on—*too much* is what he'd make of it, she told herself derisively.

'*Fate!*' she hooted robustly. 'Of course not.' Her tone was laced with a shade of indignation. What sort of silly woman did he think she was? 'You live here, then?' She recalled he never had got around to telling her what he did for a living. He didn't look much like her idea of a farmer, but then what did she, the ultimate townie, know?

'No, just helping out for a few weeks.'

A casual farm labourer! This possibility seemed even more unlikely than the first option. She'd had him pegged as someone who, even if he didn't give orders, *definitely* didn't take them off anyone. To her there seemed something of the maverick about him.

Her own father had always been proud of his humble beginnings as the son of a coalminer and it struck her forcibly that he'd be ashamed if he knew his own daughter nurtured snobbish preconceptions about manual labourers. Just because a man used his muscles to earn a crust didn't mean he didn't have a brain, and if she needed proof she only had to look as far as this man. Those extraordinary eyes of his held a biting degree of intelligence.

If her friend's reports were anything to go by, babies

were expensive creatures, and most of those households who were frequently pleading poverty brought in two hefty professional salaries. This man had a child to bring up alone and, it seemed, no professional qualifications. Under the circumstances he couldn't afford to be picky about work. It must be hard worrying about money and coping with parenthood, she reflected. He faced problems every day she couldn't begin to understand; her soft heart swelled with empathy. It made her feel guilty when she considered her own comparative embarrassment of worldly riches.

'*Helping!* Is that what you call it?' A large young man with a lilting accent and a head of shocking red hair jeered as he came up behind Josh and thumped him good-naturedly on the back. 'Slacking more like, man.' He laughed. He looked with interest at Flora, his bold eyes admiring. 'Fast worker, aren't you?' he added slyly to Josh in a soft voice.

Flora fell back on her frozen routine, but frustratingly neither man appeared to notice. Josh gave a tolerant, unembarrassed smile.

'Geraint, this is Flora.' He casually performed the introductions. 'She's staying in the village. Flora, this big bull is Geraint Jones.'

'The heir apparent,' Geraint told her, swaggering in an inoffensive way. 'You going to actually do any work to-day, Josh?' he added sarcastically, jumping into a tractor and revving up the engine. 'See you later, *cariad*,' he called to Flora. 'And remember, if you want any real work done I'm your man,' he boasted. 'Now, if you want a bit of sissy painting...' he taunted, driving noisily off.

It was similar to an encounter with a bulldozer. 'Is he always so...?'

'Always, but a bit more so when a beautiful woman is around.'

She'd been called beautiful so often it didn't even register now, so why were her lower limbs suddenly afflicted by a debilitating weakness?

'You paint? I mean, that's your real trade?' An idea, probably not a good one, was occurring to her. It would be foolish to blurt anything out before she'd considered the implications of her inspiration.

'You could say that,' Josh confirmed a shade cautiously.

Flora was so excited by the brilliance of her idea that she decided that she'd throw caution to the winds.

'Well, I don't know what your schedule's like at the moment...?'

'Flexible,' he responded honestly.

'Well, I might be able to put some work your way. My friend Claire,' she explained hurriedly, 'the one who is letting me use her cottage—she asked me to find someone to redecorate the small bedroom in the cottage while I'm here. It's really dark and poky and she's just had a baby...Emily...' On anyone else Josh would have called that soft, fleeting little smile sentimental. 'And she wants the room redone before she comes up at Christmas. If you're interested...'

'You're offering me a job?' He was looking at her oddly.

'You wouldn't be working for me,' she informed him, anxious to make this point quite clear from the outset. 'I'm only acting as an agent for Claire.'

'Decorating a bedroom? You want me to decorate a bedroom?'

Flora glared. Was it such a revolutionary notion? Hadn't he decorated a bedroom before? Anyone would think she'd said something funny. She hadn't expected or wanted gratitude but he looked as though he was about to fall about laughing.

Maybe it was a male pride thing, she pondered. He might not like people, especially a woman, to know he was strapped for cash. She tried to see it from his point of view and had to concede it was possible she was coming over a bit lady bountiful.

'If you're too busy...'

'Aren't you afraid I'll kiss you again?'

She didn't see the question coming until it hit her dead centre; it completely threw her off balance. *Aren't you more afraid he won't?* the sly inner voice silkily suggested.

Taking a deep breath, she made emergency repairs on her shattered poise. Her slender shoulders lifted casually. 'I hardly think that's likely,' she scoffed laughingly. 'I'm aware it was just a...'

One dark brow quirked enquiringly as she searched for words. Flora flushed.

'A momentary impulse,' she choked resentfully.

'Aberration, even,' he agreed soothingly.

She frowned at him with irritation; she knew deliberate provocation when she heard it. She needed to knock this kissing thing on the head once and for all.

'For your information, I've just broken up with my fiancé; kissing isn't on my agenda.'

'Why did you do that?'

Flora looked at him blankly.

'Break up with your fiancé, that is.'

Flora glared at him. 'None of your damned business,' she declared hotly.

'Sorry,' he sympathised with a patently false sincerity that set her teeth on edge. 'Sensitive subject.'

'Not at all sensitive!' she snapped immediately. 'Paul asked me to make a choice and I didn't make the one he expected.' Paul had been astonished when she had failed to see how imperative it was for her to distance herself from her disgraced father. His astonishment had eventually turned to anger at what he perceived as her selfishness. 'Also,' she added with feeling, 'he was a prize prat!'

'In fact,' Josh drawled, his eyes on her mutinous, flushed face, 'it was a normal, mutually amicable parting.'

'I'm just trying to explain why kissing isn't high on my agenda just now, so you can rest easy,' she told him, regretting her outburst.

She couldn't help recalling that kissing her had not exactly made him happy the first time, so he probably wouldn't want to again. She remembered the bleak expression in his eyes as he'd made that extraordinary statement. If he really hadn't kissed anyone for some time that meant he had a whole lot of sexual frustration to get rid of. She didn't want to be his therapy. Although, she conceded, letting her eyes roam at will for one self-indulgent moment over his sleekly powerful body, there would be fringe benefits! It was almost enough to make a girl sorry she wasn't into shallow and superficial relationships.

'Ah, you're afraid of the rebound thing...?'

Her teeth clenched. Was he jumping to all the wrong conclusions deliberately? She met his eyes—you bet he was, she concluded instantly. There was no mistaking the fact he was enjoying her discomfiture. He'd probably taken delight in depriving flies of their wings when he was a little boy.

'There's absolutely no prospect of me rebounding in *your* direction!'

'You mean you don't encourage the hired help to take liberties. This isn't actually about being off men in general, just a particular category of men, for which read those without the fancy cars, fancy clothes and fancy salaries to match.' His voice was coldly derisive.

He made her feel so guiltily defensive that she almost began searching her conscience until she realised that, whatever other faults she had, she had never judged people by their bank balances, although she knew plenty of people that did.

'Are you implying I'm a snob?'

He considered the heated accusation. 'I don't know you well enough to imply anything—yet,' he qualified.

Flora didn't like that little contemplative smile that accompanied the qualification one little bit. For starters it made her pulse-rate do slightly scary things.

'Do you want the job?' she snapped, already regretting her silly altruism. The man had got by before she'd come along; it wasn't as though he looked malnourished or anything—far from it!

Josh looped his thumbs in the loops of his waistband and looked thoughtful. 'What's it pay?'

'Pay!' she echoed in a startled voice.

'You didn't expect me to do it for free, did you?'

Her lips tightened at the sarcasm; he really did have a knack of making her feel embarrassed and just ever so slightly stupid. If anything, she normally played down her intellect in front of men; for some reason this one made her feel positively inadequate!

'Of course I didn't. I just hadn't thought...' God, what happened to detached and businesslike? I sound like a real pea brain! She cleared her throat and tried to retrieve the situation. 'What's the going rate?' she enquired briskly.

He named a figure and she nodded sagely.

'That sounds fair,' she agreed gravely. She didn't know what she was talking about and she suspected he knew it. If he was trying to rip her off she'd have to make up the excess from her own pocket; she couldn't make Claire suffer financially because she wasn't prepared to admit her ignorance in front of this man.

'That's a deal, then.' He approached her, hand extended.

Flora stared at the strong hand as if it were a snake. As she tentatively placed her own in his the scent of his warm body reached her nostrils. She tried not breathing but the faint musky smell still made her stomach muscles twang like the entire string section of an orchestra. The unseasonably hot day wasn't entirely responsible for the sweat that trickled slowly down between her breasts.

He didn't shake her hand, instead he raised it to his lips in a gesture that should have been absurd, only she felt no desire to laugh at all...melt, well, yes...that was another thing entirely!

He lifted his head and looked directly into her eyes; the expression in those silvery depths was explicitly sensual. It was at that second that she knew exactly how big a mistake she'd made in virtually inviting the man into her home!

Calm down, Flora, she told herself firmly as her heart-rate rocketed. Think worst scenario: you bump into him—not literally, of course—occasionally. She stubbornly worked around images that wouldn't quite clear from her head of several interesting varieties of collisions she could have with Josh Prentice. She bit back a horrified whimper.

Cope, of course she could cope! She hadn't reached her advanced years without being able to survive mentally and emotionally intact the odd bit of sexual craving. She could cope with anything. She was going to fill her lungs with gallons of fresh country air! Wholesome, emotionally untaxing pursuits like walking the hills and talking to the odd sheep were going to fill her days, not steamy daydreams.

'If you have other commitments,' she began hopefully,

putting her tingling hand behind her back and rubbing it against the soft wool of her sweater. 'It might be more convenient for you to decorate the nursery after I've left.'

'And when would that be?'

'I'm not entirely sure yet.' Dad didn't want her to visit while he was in the programme.

'You must have very understanding bosses.'

Flora smiled vaguely and didn't explain that since she'd been made a partner last year she was one of the bosses. Actually her colleagues had been incredibly supportive throughout the ordeal of the trial.

'There's actually no hurry or anything.'

'It's very considerate of you to worry about my welfare.'

Flora didn't feel considerate, she felt cornered!

'But I'm quite adept at juggling more than one task.'

This boast drew a small, wry grin from Flora. 'Not like any men I've met, then,' she snorted.

'No,' he mused with an arrogantly confident smile. 'I think you'll find I'm actually not like any other man you've met.' His voice flowed over her like warm, rich molasses.

Flora swallowed nervously and dabbed the tiny pinpricks of sweat that beaded her upper lip with the tip of her tongue.

His grey eyes zoomed in on the nervous gesture; his nostrils flared. 'Besides,' he continued hoarsely, 'we won't be here long.'

'You mean you and Liam don't live here? I assumed... Do you move around a lot?'

'A man has to go where the work is.'

His hard, emotionless statement confirmed her initial suspicions concerning his finances and she was glad she'd been able to put some work his way, even though he was a very hard man to relax around.

'That must be hard with a child,' she sympathised softly.

'You disapprove.' His lip lifted in a faint sneer as he pounced on this evidence of her judgemental nature with relish.

'I'm no judge of such things—' and never would be if her track record so far was anything to go by, she thought gloomily '—but Liam looked a pretty happy, well-adjusted child to me.'

'You'll find out when you have one of your own that all kids have a little bit of the Jekyll and Hyde in them.'

The idea of having a child of her own brought about an odd, achy sensation—had her biological clock swung into action early? she wondered. At twenty-seven she'd always considered she had plenty of time to think about children.

'That presupposes I want some of my own.'

'And you don't.' His expression seemed to suggest he wasn't surprised.

'I didn't say that,' she countered crossly. 'I just don't like it when people make assumptions. Besides, call me an old-fashioned girl, but I think it sensible to think about babies after I find a suitable father for them.'

'Paul the prat wasn't keen on kids, then,' he sympathised.

'Paul,' she felt goaded into rashly revealing, 'requires *all* the proper accessories in his life.' Her lips acquired a cynical twist as she considered Paul's priorities. He'd probably have expected her to time the pregnancies to coincide with election years; a baby or a pregnant wife must be good for the odd vote or two.

'It sounds like the perfect match to me. You look like an accessory sort of lady yourself.' He was looking appraisingly at her very expensive clothes.

'You do insults amazingly well, Mr Prentice.' Flora's nostrils flared. 'Strangely, I don't feel inclined to discuss my shallowness just now.'

'You remembered my name…eventually, and it's Josh.'

Truth be told, she remembered everything about him including the expert way he kissed. 'Your name, but not how offensive you are, obviously,' she hissed, 'or I wouldn't have offered you the job.'

'I wondered how long the "I'm not the boss just the agent" line would last,' he fired back with a cynical sneer. 'I suppose you're going to be watching everything I do, stifling my artistic freedom…'

The sheer bloody-minded silliness of this accusation ought to have made her laugh, but it didn't. Did he take his shirt off indoors too? Perspiration prickled over her entire body as for the duration of a single heartbeat she contemplated what watching this man at work would do to her indiscriminate hormones. It made her bones ache just thinking about it.

'Nothing,' she told him, her voice shaking with sincerity, 'could be further from the truth and you can let your artistic inclinations run wild,' she promised recklessly.

'Every man has his price,' he admitted solemnly. 'That sounded suspiciously like an offer I can't refuse.'

He made it sound as though she'd been begging for his professional services. 'That's…that's marvellous,' she responded weakly.

'I'll make a start tomorrow.'

'That soon!'

Her spontaneous dismay made his lips twitch. 'Before you change your mind.'

'I wouldn't go back on a deal, despite provocation…' she told him, angrily defending her integrity. The man somehow managed to twist everything she said to his own advantage. With that marketable ability combined with his indisputable physical attributes—which, sad though it was, *did* make a difference—she was amazed he hadn't found a lucrative niche somewhere. 'I think you're in the wrong job,' she reflected drily.

'You're not alone there.' He grinned wryly, recalling how horrified his family had been when he'd turned his back on the academic avenues open to him and announced his intention of becoming an artist. They'd come around now, of course; success made a lot of things acceptable.

'You should use your natural talents.'

He looked struck by the idea. 'Like kissing, you mean,' he suggested with a hungry-tiger smirk.

'Why,' she ejaculated, 'do you keep bringing that up?' Her teeth hurt as she ground them yet again.

'Because it's on your mind, not to mention mine…? Yes,' he confirmed, giving the subject some thought, 'that's it. I keep thinking about kissing you.' His jaw tightened. It was true and unforgivable: when he ought to be concentrating on other more vital issues his mind kept returning to that single brief, unsatisfactory kiss.

His resentful glare suggested it was all her fault—the cheek of the man—and typical of men, full stop!

'Why? Do I look like your wife? Do I remind you of her or something?'

Flora was so shocked to hear the words leave her lips she gave a horrified gasp and pressed a belated silencing hand over her mouth. True, this question had been nagging away at her since yesterday, but, assuming she'd never see him again, she hadn't thought she'd ever have the opportunity to ask him, or for that matter the lack of judgement to do so!

Josh had gone very still. Flora started when he slowly began to move towards her. Her attention was riveted by

KIM LAWRENCE 45

the graceful, lithe way he moved, beautiful but almost menacing. His blank expression told her zero about his intentions, but as he came closer she could see the slashing angle of his chiselled cheekbones seemed more pronounced and a solitary muscle pumped in his lean cheek.

He stopped just in front of her and, reaching out, took her chin in one hand and swept it upwards. His eyes swept dispassionately over her beautiful oval face; he seemed to be unmoved by what he saw.

Flora didn't move; she couldn't. Sexual anticipation mingled with mind-numbing apprehension inside her, creating sheer havoc. Wide-eyed, she watched as he slowly shook his dark head firmly from side to side, never for one instant releasing her from the merciless grip of his gaze. Despite the relentless intensity of that stare she couldn't shake the conviction that he somehow wasn't actually seeing her, perhaps it was the face of his lost love, little Liam's mother, he saw.

'No, you're nothing like her.' His voice was harsh. *'Nothing!'* he added as if he couldn't emphasise this point too much.

Flora felt a shaft of relief quiver through her. It mattered, she wasn't quite sure why, but his reply had mattered a lot to her.

'She wasn't a blonde.' His eyes touched the silver strands clustered around her face. 'But then who's to say you are?'

'I think I'm the definitive expert on that subject.'

His hand dropped away and a sudden devilish grin abruptly banished the brooding shadows from his expression. 'You have no idea how tempted I am to say prove it,' he suddenly confessed.

'Restrain yourself!' She sniffed, wondering how she ought to go about distracting him from this ticklish subject.

'If I kissed you now would it constitute a sacking offence?'

Flora's heart turned over in the confined space of her tight chest. As shock seeped steadily through her she caught her breath raggedly and her hot colour faded of its own accord, leaving her pale.

The expression *perfectly pale* flitted through Josh's head as he feasted his eyes on the delicate symmetry of her clear-cut features, resting the longest on the full curve of her softly sumptuous lips. His bold, sensual survey made the blood pound noisily in her ears.

Some dim memory of self-preservation told Flora she ought to summon some cutting witticism that would cool his ardour and cut him down to size. After all, didn't she have enough in her repertoire to suit any occasion?

As she met the smouldering intensity of his speculative gaze the memory flickered and died. Truth told, there was nothing in the world she wanted more than to be kissed by and kiss Josh Prentice. The admission cost her what little sense of what was appropriate she had left. Honesty, even with yourself, *especially* with yourself, wasn't always the best policy!

'You can't get sacked from a job you haven't started yet,' she breathed huskily.

'You've a fine legal mind,' he admired, placing his hands on her shoulders.

'You're not looking at my mind,' she felt impelled to point out.

'You noticed that, did you?' His thumb made a backwards sweeping movement over the generous curve of her full lips. Her lips parted under the gentle pressure.

'It's hard to miss.' His dark face was swimming in and out of focus; the desire to be kissed was so intense she felt actually faint.

'So are your lips,' he rasped throatily. 'They really are quite, *quite* perfect. Very sexy,' he added, brushing her lips lightly with his own. 'Very sensual.' Another butterfly caress accompanied his observation. 'Very kissable,' he rasped, his voice dropping to a soft, sexy whisper.

'*Josh,*' she almost whimpered his name as his tongue flickered out to touch the moist softness of her inner lip. Her hands grasped helplessly at empty space before finally clutching at his broad, bare shoulders. His skin was warm, faintly moist and satisfyingly smooth. She could feel the faintest quiver of tightening muscles under her hands.

'Yes, angel...?'

The scent of his body made her senses spin and increased her growing sense of frustration. 'Will you kiss me properly?'

His breath whistled in a low sibilant hiss. 'Try and stop me,' he growled.

Such a thing never even entered her head. If she hadn't responded to the pressure of his lips with such spectacular enthusiasm the kiss might have stayed controlled. As it was she plastered herself against him in an entirely wanton manner, aided and abetted in her task by the steely arm that snaked around her just beneath her ribcage.

She automatically opened her mouth fully to intensify the erotic exploration of his thrusting tongue. Her co-operation became almost frenzied as her fingers sank deep into his luxuriant dark hair. With growing urgency her trembling fingertips moved over the strong contours of his face. He turned his head and caught one finger in his mouth. Holding her eyes with his smouldering gaze, he began slowly to suckle.

It was all too much. Flora's knees buckled. She would have stumbled and fallen if he hadn't supported her.

The cold nose of a curious farm dog pressed against her

leg made her start. She looked down into the liquid brown eyes of the Border collie and groaned. 'Oh, God,' she gasped, 'this is stupid!' She pulled free of his arms and he didn't try and prevent her.

'On a spectacular scale, probably,' he conceded. 'But who gives a damn?'

His light-hearted response drew a reluctant laugh from her. 'Call me hemmed in by convention, but me, actually. Also I wouldn't want to be responsible for you getting the sack.' Feeling painfully awkward, she tucked the hem of her shirt back in the waistband of her trousers.

She couldn't quite get her head around her swift and total surrender; it made her pulses go haywire just thinking about those wildly erotic moments. Josh had kissed like a starving man, which wasn't surprising considering he must have been repressing the sensual side—and he did have a *very* sensual side—of his nature since his wife's death.

Obviously she'd be a fool to read anything deeper in his desire for her. She half wished she were into self-delusion—it would be quite a nice illusion to imagine there was anything remotely resembling a future in any relationship she embarked on with this man. How could it...? He was still in love with his wife!

'What time is it?' he suddenly asked sharply.

Still distracted, disorientated and plagued by all manner of mystifying aches, she glanced at the slim face of her wrist watch. 'Almost three.'

'Hell!' Josh cursed. 'I promised I'd do the fencing before teatime. A rain check, then,' he suggested casually.

Flora found she resented deeply his self-composure when hers had deserted her totally. She wasn't used to men who automatically took her compliance for granted and it was pretty obvious it hadn't even occurred to him she'd refuse. Flora forgot she no longer had a mane of hair to swish and made the flicking motion with her chin that would have sent the swirling mass backwards. I'll have to come up with an equally effective distracting gesture to give me breathing space or people will start thinking I've got a nervous tic.

'Tomorrow, then.'

Flora blinked. It was a masterly dismissal; she was having a bigger problem than ever seeing him taking orders.

'Maybe, I'll leave the key under the doormat if I'm not home.'

'Sure.' His smile seemed to say he knew full well she'd be home but he was prepared to humour her.

The spectacular scenery was totally wasted on Flora during the rest of her walk back to the cottage.

CHAPTER THREE

'Is ANYONE home?' Josh pushed open the ajar kitchen door.

'Thank goodness!' Flora breathed thankfully. She gestured urgently with her tightly balled fists. 'Don't just stand there, come in…come in!' she hissed.

Josh had been prepared for a cosmetic display of coolness—just at first, of course; he was fairly confident that Flora would thaw quite quickly—but *this*! He walked over the threshold and saw immediately that her urgency had very little to do with a compelling desire for his body.

'Well, don't just stand there!' she told him in an agonised whisper. 'Do something!'

'*Me!* You've got the…' Brows raised, he looked at the metal implement clenched in one white-knuckled fist. 'What is that, anyhow? A poker?' Whatever it was it looked lethal and more than up to the task of disposing of a rodent a lot bigger than the small defenceless one she had cornered—or was it the other way around…?

It made quite a picture. He strove to maintain a solemn expression; if Fleet Street's best had only known what it took to shake the cool and collected Miss Graham.

His bland tone made Flora want to scream. Why wasn't the stupid man responding with the urgency the situation demanded?

'I hardly think that's relevant,' she told him, still without taking her eyes off the small, frozen figure of a field mouse. Her toes curled with disgust in her blue furry slippers.

'Bash it or something,' he suggested.

Flora gave an exasperated sigh. 'If I could have,' she pointed out witheringly, 'don't you think I already would have? I just can't kill things.' She confessed this failing with a wail from between clenched teeth.

'Then let it go,' he suggested. One glance told him the little rodent wasn't going anywhere while they were here. It was literally frozen with fear, half a breath away from heart failure—and it wasn't alone, he thought, his scrutiny switching to Flora who was giving a good impression of a statue if you discounted the odd tremor or two. He had to concede she made quite a striking statue; she reminded him of one of those long-legged impossibly graceful Degas figures, except her skin wasn't cold bronze, it was creamy white, soft and... He cleared his throat noisily and transferred his attention to the intruder.

'What?' she yelped. 'And stay awake another night hearing it scratching under the floorboards—not on your life!'

'You want me to bash it, is that it?'

She looked at him for the first time, her big blue reproachful eyes screaming heartless monster. 'No...no!' she responded miserably.

'Well, make up your mind.' Female logic was enough to drive a man to drink.

Flora suddenly had an inspirational thought. 'Couldn't you put it outside...? Not near the house, though.'

'Let me get this straight. You want me to remove the mouse, pat it on the head and tell it to go find another residence.' So what if the heartless woman had a soft spot for furry things and children? He wasn't going to let that influence him. It was possible Lucrezia Borgia used to get mushy about babies. It was essential he didn't start getting sucked in by her act; he had to remember why he was here.

The popular theory amongst those who knew him well was that when they handed out the obstinacy Josh had got a second helping.

'In essence, yes, and sooner would be better than later.'

Flora couldn't look as he bent over to scoop up the tiny terrified creature. Her entire body sagged with relief as she heard him leave the room. It was gone. She sank down into a cheerfully painted kitchen chair and let out a long, shuddering sigh. It was only a few minutes before he returned and Flora was already geared up to defend her pathetic behaviour.

'I know it was more scared of me,' she assured him, determined to get the first word in before any of that mockery in his eyes could find its way to his lips. Her stomach went into a clenching routine she was getting familiar with by now. Why does every thought I have about this man have to include his mouth? 'I know it was a stereotypical female reaction...' she croaked.

'I don't know, you didn't climb on a chair,' he conceded.

Only because my knees were shaking too hard. 'Thanks for that,' she responded drily. 'I already feel a complete idiot.'

'I can't imagine why,' he drawled.

'I don't actually have a thing about mice.'

'I'm glad you explained that or I might have gone on thinking you were phobic.'

She gave him a frosty glare. 'It's that horrid scratchy noise they make—' she gave a tiny shudder '—and they're dirty.' He couldn't argue that point. 'Speaking of which, hadn't you better wash your hands?'

'You've not got some cleanliness fetish too?' he enquired suspiciously. His eyes skimmed the cluttered work surface and he shook his head. 'I see you've not.'

'It's hardly kind to call someone a slob when they're in a traumatised condition,' she informed him severely. 'I was in the middle of making my breakfast when that…'

'Wild beast leapt out at you.'

'You can laugh!' Her pout quivered into a reluctant grin. 'If you hadn't come along I'm not sure what I'd have done next.'

'I was wondering that myself,' he admitted. 'In a war of attrition the tough survive; I suppose it depends on how tough you are?'

Flora's expression hardened as her mind automatically drifted back over the last weeks. 'Tough enough when necessary,' she assured him grimly.

'I believe you.' He turned from the sink and, shaking his wet hands, looked expectantly at her.

Flora got to her feet, extracted a clean towel from a drawer and handed it to him. 'Well, thanks, you may be a sarcastic pig, but you were handy.' She sniffed.

His comprehensive scrutiny of her person recalled her a little belatedly to the fact she was still dressed only in a light robe which gaped revealingly down the front to display a large quantity of her short silky slip nightdress and an even larger quantity of bare leg. Trying not to act as if his eyes didn't make her want to crawl out of her hot skin, she casually belted the robe around her middle—perhaps *too* casually because he looked mildly amused by her action.

He was wearing jeans as he had the day before but this pair was more disreputable with large jagged tears in the knees, his white tee shirt was clean and nicely pressed but permanently stained with large multi-coloured blotches of paint. The thin fabric clung, giving more than a mere suggestion of his muscle-packed torso. Overalls would have been more professional, she decided disapprovingly. A tent might be even better, an acidly derisive voice in her head added, and a lot less revealing. If she was honest with herself Flora knew that even if he wore a paper bag over his head it wouldn't deter her lustful and lurid imagination.

'What are you doing here at such an ungodly hour?' she grumbled, unhappily acknowledging that all the determination in the world couldn't prevent her reacting at some basic instinctual level to this man—in short she fancied him like hell! Unfortunately, an equally strong gut instinct told her, it would all end in tears, as her granny, had she had one, might have said.

'Ungodly!' he echoed derisively. 'The day's half over, woman. At least,' he qualified, 'it is if you've been up since five.'

'Who looks after Liam while you work?' she wondered out loud.

'Oh, he's having a whale of a time. Megan dotes on him—for some mystifying reason she can't get enough of him.'

Did that go for the father as well as the son? Flora wondered darkly. Could this mysterious Megan, whom he hadn't seen fit to mention before, be just as keen to get her hands on Josh? She didn't like the sound of this Celtic temptress one little bit.

'*Megan*...?' She heard the sharp tone in her voice and had no trouble detecting a shrill thread of pure, unadulterated green-eyed monster! What made this mortifying discovery even harder to swallow was the strong probability that Josh too had heard and was even now drawing the exact same conclusion she was—it wasn't as if he was exactly slow or unaware of his own charms!

Determined to bluff this out if she died in the effort, she lifted her chin up and pinned a suitably disinterested expression on her face. If he *dared* to suggest she was doing anything other than making polite chit-chat...! She could fake it as well as anybody; at least, she could normally. The fact that Josh Prentice's presence seemed to seriously inhibit certain essential social skills increased her panicky feelings.

'What a lovely name,' she gushed insincerely.

'I think so,' Josh murmured pleasantly. He bit back a complacent grin as her sickly smile slipped slightly. 'You must meet her—I feel sure you'd get on.'

'I can't wait. But actually I didn't come here to socialise.'

'Why exactly did you come here?'

Josh saw wariness slide into her blue eyes before they slid away from his completely.

'I thought I'd already told you my fiancé and I recently split up.'

He struck the side of his head with his open-palmed hand. 'How could I forget? Paul the prat! So you're here to lick your wounds and recover from your emotional devastation,' he drawled sarcastically.

She ground her teeth and glared at him in open dislike. Why doesn't he just come out and say I'm a hard cow!

'Not everybody parades their feelings for the world to see!' she snapped.

He carefully folded the towel and handed it back to her. When she went to take it he didn't let go. 'Not everyone *has* emotions to parade,' he taunted softly.

Her eyes sparkling with temper, Flora snatched the towel free after a short and undignified tussle.

'You don't expect me to believe you were actually in love with this guy! Oh, I'm sure he had a lot to recommend him, like moving in the right social circles, and call me intuitive or just plain psychic, but was he by any chance loaded?' His languid smile grew closer to a sneer as her bosom continued to heave dramatically and her eyes filled with tears of anger.

'I don't give a damn what you believe!' she gritted back defiantly.

He made her engagement sound shallow and calculating—he obviously thought she was both. In fact Paul had never actually proposed, so there had been no specific moment when she'd had to come to a decision; it had just been something he and their family and friends had taken for granted would eventually happen. And Flora herself, when she'd thought about it, hadn't been able to come up with a single reason why they shouldn't get married!

She wanted children eventually, and she'd never enjoyed the meat market that passed for the singles scene, and as for waiting for the *one true love thing*, she was far too old and worldly wise for such nonsense. Besides, she'd seen close to what loving someone too much could do if that special someone was taken from you. If that sort of loss could destroy someone as strong as her father, what chance would she have?

'Well, what am I to think? You didn't exactly fight me off with a stick, did you...? Hardly the actions of a woman who loves someone else.'

No, she hadn't, and in not doing so she'd laid herself wide open to this sort of derision. She silently cursed the hormonal insanity responsible for her wanton behaviour. 'That's because sex has nothing to do with emotions.' Here's wishing...she thought wistfully.

'That's a very masculine point of view.'

Flora found the creamy skin of her throat where his eyes had touched was tingling. She resisted the temptation to lift a hand to protect that vulnerable area from his gaze.

Happily her breathing had returned to something that would pass for normal; Flora gave a sigh of relief. 'It's a man's world,' she reminded him calmly. 'I find a girl gets on much better if she lives her life by their standards,' she claimed brazenly.

'In fact, you're one of this new breed of female who can drink as hard and curse as hard as any man. *Impressive!* I'm not knocking it; I can see the advantages. Seduction would be so much simpler, not to mention cheaper, if a man could dispense with flowers and romantic dinners, if he could just say do you fancy a...'

'You're about as romantic as a hole in the head!' she flung angrily at him. Her eyes narrowed and she threw the towel still clutched in her hands in the linen basket, wishing with all her heart that this infuriating man could be disposed of so easily. The man had a positive genius for misrepresenting *everything* she said.

'I suppose *you* think nature arranged it for men to have fun spreading their oats while women stay at home darning their smelly socks.' She looked on resentfully as he threw back his head and laughed; it was a rich, deep, uninhibited sound. 'What,' she enquired frigidly, 'is so funny?'

He wiped the moisture from the corner of his eyes, which she discovered crinkled in a deeply delightful way when he laughed.

'The idea of you darning a sock, that's what,' he told her. 'In fact, I'd eat mine if you even knew what a darning needle looks like.'

'It was a figure of speech; nobody darns socks these days.'

'Megan probably does,' he mused thoughtfully.

'Then she sounds the perfect mate for you,' she snarled back nastily. 'A doormat.'

'I know it brings out the matchmaker in most people to see a single father, but I'm not actually interested in finding a mate.' He was gambling that she was the sort of woman who couldn't resist a challenge and hopefully not him either. He firmly quashed unspecific feelings of unease. It wasn't as if there was any law that said you couldn't enjoy revenge!

'Does Megan know this?' she hissed unpleasantly.

'Megan's already married,' he admitted sadly. 'To Huw.'

'Huw?'

'Geraint's father. You remember Geraint—the young farmer, big bloke, very eager to sow his share of oats. Megan is his mother.'

'Oh.'

'I don't know why you're jealous, you know you're the only woman I want to kiss.' Self-loathing darkened his deep-set eyes and robbed the statement of flattery. Even so, Flora found his words tugged at her senses, producing a dangerous drowsy dreaminess.

Now his libido had come out of its grief-induced coma, Flora doubted he was going to be satisfied with one woman for long. She might be the first but she had no illusions about being the last. This was one good reason not to go any further down this particular path. In theory the uncomplicated 'sex of the safe variety is harmless' line worked fine! In practice the whole thing was an emotional minefield she didn't want to negotiate.

'I'm not the jealous type, never have been.' She gave a happy carefree trill of laughter—at least, it was meant to be carefree; unfortunately it emerged as shrill. 'Don't let me hold you back if you want to get on with your work,' she told him pointedly. She proceeded to make loud bustling noises with the crockery messily spread out on the work surface.

'It's traditional to offer tradesmen a cup of tea before

they actually commence work,' he remonstrated mockingly. 'Don't you know *anything*?'

'Apparently not,' she responded drily. The kitchen was too small to contain such a large man without inducing a strong feeling of claustrophobia. She wiped her damp palms along the sides of her wrap. 'Any other rules I should know?'

'The tea should be supplied at regular intervals throughout the working day.' He bent his head and she felt the warm brush of his breath against her earlobe. 'The next is just a little personal foible of mine...' His intimate husky whisper trickled over her like warm honey.

Weak-kneed, her body swayed slightly and he stepped forward to provide the support she needed. The fit was remarkably snug, she decided as their respective curves and angles slotted neatly together. She couldn't help imagining how it would feel if they got even closer. Her aching breasts felt heavy and swollen as they chafed against the thin fabric of her nightdress.

'What would that foible be?' she enquired huskily. Actually, she thought maybe she knew; standing this close it was impossible not to notice that he was in an aroused state. A bone-deep excitement rose up from some secret, previously untapped reservoir within her. The ferocity of her response to his arousal was almost frightening. Her busy hands slowly stilled; the sexual tension in the air around them was so thick she could have taken a knife and still had trouble slicing through it.

Turning around might constitute encouragement, but what the hell? she decided recklessly! There was only just so much a woman could take!

Josh looked down into her expectant, delicately flushed face; there was nothing coy about the way she was looking at him. There was no banner saying, 'Take me!' but that slumbrously sexy invitation was just as explicit. She was quite simply breathtaking in her tousled, not-long-out-of-bed state. Thinking of her in bed set off a train of thought that exacerbated the persistent ache in his groin.

His throat muscles visibly worked overtime as he swallowed hard. 'Biscuits,' he told her flatly. 'Preferably chocolate. If the old blood sugar takes a nosedive I'm worse than useless.'

One second she could almost taste the kiss, the next all she could taste was the bitter bile of humiliation. One shocked blink and the sexual glaze cleared from Flora's eyes. She gave a tiny gasp and, cheeks burning with mortification, tried to turn away.

'Whoa!' Josh soothed. Taking her by the elbow, he restrained her bid for escape. 'I was joking.'

And since when couldn't I take a joke or rejection? she asked herself. Maybe since the joke included not being kissed by Josh—is that desperate or what? Tiny pinpricks of blood dotted her lower lip as she released the pressure of her teeth. Her hectic breathing gradually slowed. Soothed slightly, and feeling deeply embarrassed, she stopped struggling and stood passively.

'Poor joke?' he suggested woodenly.

Either he had got cold feet at the last minute or he got his kicks from seeing women squirm; if so he must be a very happy man... A quick upwards glance told her he didn't look happy.

'I think maybe I'm the joke. I came onto you like a...' She found there was a limit to how far she could take the brutal honesty route, even though it seemed a bit late to act as if nothing had happened, but if she was being strictly accurate she supposed nothing had. Perhaps that was why she was hurting so much...? She cleared her throat. 'But you did do your share of encouragement.'

'Did you come here to torment me or decorate the nursery?' she wondered bluntly.

A maverick nerve leapt in his cheek. 'The torment is a two-way thing,' he responded with equal candour.

Her expression softened. His shadowed eyes suggested he had an inner conflict at least as great as her own, and small wonder! She was so caught up in what she was feeling, she hadn't really paused to look at it from his point of view.

Did he feel he was betraying the memory of his wife by wanting another woman? This was what you got for getting involved with a man with emotional baggage.

'Call me shallow, but part of me is glad to hear you say that,' she confessed. 'It's nice to have company when you're suffering.' The self-mocking smile died from her lips and her forehead pleated in an earnest frown. She didn't want to come over as some sort of bleeding heart, but she felt she had to let him know she understood, as much as anyone who hadn't been in his shoes could, that was...

'But you mustn't feel bad about...about...' She struggled to find a word which covered the almost kiss and the high-voltage sexually charged atmosphere. She gave up. 'Sexual feelings are perfectly normal.'

Josh looked startled by her solemn announcement. The hand that had been raking his dark hair fell away.

'You really ought to talk about these things, you know,' she told him kindly, 'not bottle them up. We all have needs; it was bound to happen some time.'

Josh had been clinically pondering her sexuality since he'd met her. Well, he'd been able to fool himself it was clinical interest—at least up until this point. There was nothing intellectual about the savage impulse that made him contemplate discovering Miss Flora Graham's needs—he'd like a leisurely day or so to explore all the possibilities of that particular subject.

The savage feelings he was fighting to control seemed all the more crude because she appeared to ooze sensitivity. It was getting harder by the second to reject the possibility that she actually was sensitive, compassionate— you got exactly what you saw!

Not that he'd be getting anything if that was the case, he reminded himself heavily. The 'sins of the father' line only worked up to a point, and not at all when the son in question was a beautiful daughter who had eyes that shone with integrity, when they weren't shining with lust for him! Not just lust, there was warmth and affection there too. God, what a mess!

'Perhaps you're just not ready...emotionally speaking, for...' Hell! He'd felt pretty ready in every other way.

Thinking about the imprint of his big, sexually primed body up against her sent a gentle wave of carnation pink over her fair skin. It occurred to her that being plagued with lustful thoughts as she was made her unbiased advice a bit suspect.

'Or maybe I'm not the right person to...' she suggested bravely. 'Is it long since your wife...?' she fished delicately.

'Three years.'

'Three!' She was startled. 'But Liam must have been...'

'Bridie died during the birth, some sort of embolism.' His face could have been carved from granite as he provided the basic details.

Flora didn't wonder at the dark anger in his eyes; there was no way to rationalise such a cruel twist of fate. She thought of Liam and swallowed the emotional lump in her throat. Silently she pushed Josh down towards a kitchen chair. He co-operated and folded his big body into the inadequate seat. Flora shuffled her bottom onto the table beside him; she maintained the physical contact of her hand on his shoulder.

'That's very rare. My father's a doctor,' she added to explain the depth of her lay person's knowledge. She could feel the tension that tied his muscles in knots through her fingertips.

'I was told that it's uncommon.'

'You've brought Liam up since he was a baby?'

'We've spent one night apart. I decided on that occasion that he'd be better off without me. I ran away.' The self-recrimination in his voice was vicious. 'I sometimes think that he'd have been better off in the long run if I'd left him with Jake, he'd have a more normal family life… siblings…two parents…' In his blackest moments he still occasionally wondered if he was just being selfish…if he wasn't putting his needs ahead of Liam's.

An instinctive sound of protest escaped Flora's throat. Hadn't she seen with her own eyes what a great father Josh was? She decided she didn't like the sound of this *perfect* architect brother one bit. He probably never lost an opportunity to remind Josh how successful he was, she decided, endowing this unseen figure with an ego to match his insensitivity.

'That's rubbish!' she suddenly announced. Her outraged tone drew Josh's startled attention to her indignant pink-cheeked face. 'If it was only one night you couldn't have run far,' she concluded logically. 'Nobody expects you to behave sensibly when your world has just fallen apart!' She clasped his hand and firmly pulled it onto her lap.

'Just because your brother has a well-paid job and nice house, it doesn't mean Liam would be better off with him, so don't even think like that. You're a great father!'

Josh could have mentioned that his twin would have

been the first to agree with her. 'You think so?' What the hell? Jake's reputation could take the odd knock or two; besides, it was rather enjoyable to have Flora defending him.

'You and your wife were obviously very…I've never had that with someone,' she told him awkwardly. 'I don't know whether that makes me lucky or unlucky,' she reflected in a soft undertone. 'But I do know someone who lost his wife and he…' Her voice cracked and she swallowed hard.

Josh stared at her fingers wrapped around his and then lifted his gaze to look long and deep into her blue eyes. They were soft and misty with compassion.

'Your parents?'

She nodded. 'Mum was such a quiet person, you wouldn't think someone like that could leave such a great gaping hole in your life… I felt it, but not like Dad did. He's the strong, reliable sort, who always copes. I suppose that was the problem: everyone thought he was coping—but he wasn't. If only I'd been…'

Suddenly aware that his attention matched the intensity of her outpouring, Flora made a self-conscious meal of clearing her throat. Her eyelashes flickered downwards to shield her eyes from him.

'The point is, Josh, that he didn't cope—you have and you've brought up a beautiful boy.' There was no mistaking the depth of her admiration. 'You shouldn't knock yourself if you make mistakes, or have doubts.'

'I can't do this!' he ground out abruptly as he surged to his feet.

Flora was bewildered by the strength of his unexpected and mystifying declaration. 'What…?'

'You're definitely not the right person,' he explained harshly.

It gave Flora a brutal jolt to recognise her own words. 'Oh!' Well, she had asked. Hell! She'd even put the idea into his head to begin with. 'Well, that simplifies matters, doesn't it?' She felt physically sick with the suddenness and finality of the rejection.

A rational part of her knew she should be glad he'd saved her from making a bad mistake. How could you feel you'd lost something that had never been yours to begin with? she wondered. Ironically, she hadn't felt anything approaching this awful when Paul had announced he couldn't marry her.

Josh gave a terse nod. 'Where's the room?'

'You're still taking on the job, then?'

'Do you want me to?'

Having him around would be a kind of refined torture, but she must have some hidden masochistic streak—it was the only explanation, she concluded miserably as she found herself nodding. 'I've told Claire I found somebody and she was delighted.' Flora continued to look at some point over his left shoulder.

'Lead on, then.'

Flora gestured towards the door that concealed the narrow stairway. 'I'll leave you to it, if you don't mind. There's only two bedrooms; you want the one at the back.'

She waited until she heard his footsteps on the wooden boards above her head before she permitted the tears to seep from beneath her eyelids. Silently she allowed them to stream down her cheeks for a couple of minutes before she dashed her hand angrily across her damp cheeks. She splashed water from a cold-running tap over her no doubt blotchy face, then for good measure ducked her head under the cold stream.

She was giving a good impression of a wet dog shaking the moisture from her dripping head of hair when she became aware that Josh was standing there watching her. His quiet, still presence sent a shiver up her spine. His expression was sombre.

'In lieu of a cold shower.'

Her bluntness made him blink. 'I upset you.'

'Something like that,' Flora confirmed wryly. She wiped the excess moisture from her face with a slightly unsteady hand. 'A bit of sexual frustration never did anyone permanent damage,' she announced briskly. 'Don't look so shocked,' she snapped. 'It's not as if we both don't know what just happened.' He'd said thanks, but no, thanks, that was what had just happened and she felt a lot more than humiliation. She felt…bereft, she acknowledged wonderingly. *Why…?*

'That can't happen to you very often…you're a very desirable woman,' he added gruffly, by way of explanation.

So desirable he'd had no trouble saying no. 'I think you made the right decision,' she told him with serenity she was far from feeling. 'You've obviously got a lot of unresolved emotional issues to deal with before you take the plunge, so to speak.'

Plunge. Josh had an intense mental flash of himself plunging deeply into her receptive body. His body responded vigorously to the erotic image. His breath expelled in an audible hiss as he dragged his eyes away from her face.

Her ablutions had left a pool of water on the flagstoned floor and dotted her nightgear with dark damp patches. Josh's roving gaze was drawn irresistibly to one prominent patch which covered the uptilted peak of her left breast.

Responding belatedly, Flora wrapped a protective arm across her chest. 'This isn't a wet tee shirt competition,' she informed him icily.

A laugh was wrenched from him. 'Do you always say things like that?'

'I can't say I've ever had the occasion to make that particular accusation before.' She sniffed. 'Actually,' she conceded, 'Paul did make a passing reference to my indelicate mind when he asked for his ring back...'

'He asked for...?' Josh's expression grew openly contemptuous. 'What a...'

'Prat?' she suggested with a half-smile and a sniff. 'Paul's a politician, so he's not big on straight talking. Actually, I can be circumspect with the best of them when the occasion warrants it.' She knew she was good at keeping people at a distance and she was slow to make friends, but those she had she valued. 'But not with my friends. Not,' she added hastily, 'that you're...' She broke off, colouring uncomfortably.

'A friend?'

'I really wouldn't have made a very good politician's wife, would I?'

'Did you want to be one?'

Her shoulders lifted. 'It seemed like a good idea at the time.'

'In other circumstances I think we might have been friends...' He sounded as though he'd made an amazing discovery. 'Maybe more,' he continued in the same dazed tone. His expression hardened. 'But the circumstances...' With a snarl of frustration he turned away, giving her a fine view of his magnificent profile.

'You don't have to explain, Josh.'

Which was just as well because he couldn't. 'Believe you me, Flora, you're better off without me.'

Flora would have liked to dispute this, but that just might have constituted grovelling and so far she'd stopped short of that—*just*. She'd like it to stay that way. She had never chased a man in her life. What was it, she wondered as he closed the door firmly behind him, that made her want to alter the habit of a lifetime for this one? If there was a remote possibility he could make it any clearer that he didn't want her, she didn't think she was up to hearing it!

CHAPTER FOUR

IT WAS after three in the morning before Flora finally reached the cottage. She'd taken at least three wrong turnings on her journey back from the Holyhead ferry, which at a conservative estimate had probably added a good forty miles to her trip.

Well, at least she could be sure she wasn't going to stumble across Josh and that, after all, had been the idea behind her day trip to Dublin. He'd worked on the nursery for several hours the day before, but all they'd exchanged before she'd taken herself off to walk the rain-soaked hills had been a few polite nothings. She hadn't returned until he'd been safely off the premises.

Her crop of blisters—curse the expensive new boots—had made a similar retreat today a painful prospect, though not as painful as being in close proximity to Josh all day! The day trip to Ireland had been the perfect solution, and Dublin always had been one of her favourite cities, though she'd not really been in an appreciative mood today. Hopefully Josh would have almost completed his task now and soon there would be no reason in the future for their paths to cross, she concluded. The thought failed to produce the philosophical smile she'd been working towards.

She kicked off her shoes as soon as she got through the cheery brick-red front door of the cottage. She dropped her purchases on the floor—for once retail therapy had failed to produce its usual soothing effect—and wearily began to climb the narrow stairs. Halfway up she turned back and, searching through the pile of bags she'd dropped, she extracted a large plush teddy bear with a particularly appealing face. She hugged him to her chest as she retraced her steps. She'd thought of Liam the instant she'd seen him. She just hoped Josh wouldn't read anything untoward into this spontaneous gesture—untoward such as she was being nice to the son because she wanted the father—and *how* she wanted the father! She noticed a light still shone from under the nursery door; Josh must have forgotten to switch it off.

'Oh my!' she breathed as she glanced around the door. The bare electric lightbulb revealed the most extraordinary transformation. An entranced expression on her face, she entered the room fully. The dark, poky little space had been transformed into a magical place by a series of stunning murals. Even she, a cynical twenty-seven-year-old, could almost believe she were under the water. The creatures peering out from behind rocks, emerging from seashells and peeping out of a wrecked galleon were all so vivid and real. It would give any child hours of delight just discovering all the hidden surprises in the vividly depicted underwater scenes.

She pulled back her hand when her fingers encountered slightly tacky paint. 'What a waste, teddy,' she breathed. 'He ought to be an artist,' she concluded admiringly.

'An interesting thought.'

Flora started violently and spun around. One arm braced against the doorjamb, Josh was standing there as large as life and twice as exciting; he was watching her. His powerful body blocked the entrance, or exit, depending on how you looked at it, completely. Flora was thinking exit in a big way and had been from the instant she'd heard his voice.

'I...I didn't know you...' she stuttered. 'What are you still doing here? Do you know what time it is?' Her heart was hammering so loudly he must hear it in the small silent room. Amidst the conflicting emotions his fixed stare was communicating, one remained constant: hunger—raw hunger! It sent neat toe-curling electricity surging through her tense frame and tied her stomach muscles into tortuous knots.

'I had nearly finished the job so I came back after Liam went to bed,' he explained. 'It's easier to work without distractions.' His lips curled in a thin, self-derisive smile.

Flora frantically tried to decipher this cryptic utterance. Does he mean I'm a distraction, and if he does am I a pleasant one...? Or were distractions by definition nasty? Panic had set in in a big way and her poor, beleaguered brain wasn't up to sorting out this sticky question.

'I'm sorry if I got in the way yesterday.' Flora listened to her meek little girl voice in exasperation. Why not just apologise for breathing and have done with it?

'Are you?' he ground out. Abruptly he lowered his smouldering eyes from hers and dragged a hand through his already tousled dark hair; the gesture was intensely weary. 'Brought back a friend—strange, I didn't have you pegged as a fluffy-toy sort of girl.'

Awkwardly Flora stopped clasping the teddy to her bosom; as a protective device he was pretty useless anyhow. 'I bought it for Liam,' she said, holding the toy out towards him. 'I just thought...' She gave an offhand shrug. 'I hope you don't mind...'

'Why should I mind?' He took the bear from her nervous clasp and placed him on the middle rung of a stepladder. 'Liam will love it. I've put the spare paint pots in the shed,' he told her prosaically.

The dangerous undercurrents that had had her on a knife's edge of anticipation were absent from his voice. A silly self-destructive part of her came close to regretting this. 'Is this what you had in mind?' he enquired, glancing casually at his handiwork.

'No,' she replied bluntly. 'My mind couldn't have come up with anything half as creative, it's incredible,' she confessed ruefully. 'You're obviously very talented!'

Josh watched as she slowly performed an admiring three-hundred-and-sixty-degree turn, pausing occasionally to chuckle spontaneously over some witty little detail.

He wasn't just talented but original too. Her face alight with enthusiasm, she turned back to Josh. 'Have you ever considered doing anything like this for a living?' she enquired tentatively. 'Not necessarily just murals...pictures and things.'

'My family wouldn't consider that a proper job for a grown man.'

Flora frowned disapprovingly. 'My father didn't think criminal law was a proper job for a woman,' she recalled drily. He'd sung the praises of house conveyancing to her on many an occasion; anything was preferable in her parents' eyes to their only child mingling with the criminal classes. 'But it didn't stop me.' She stopped, aware that her words might well have come over a bit self-congratulatory. 'Not that the two cases are similar, of course...' She hastened to assure him she could see his dilemma. 'I mean, obviously I didn't have a child to support.'

'Actually my family have been a lot of help in that direction.' Josh sent a silent apology to his nearest and dearest for creating the illusion they were a load of ignorant oafs. 'And I have imposed upon them shamelessly— once, that is,' he conceded drily, 'I got past the stage when I had to prove I could do everything a mother could only better, with one hand tied behind my back for good measure. I think they call it overcompensation,' he concluded.

His flippant words obviously covered what had been a hard time. If she contemplated for too long the poignant picture in her head of a bereaved and hurting Josh bringing up a baby all alone she'd be in floods of completely uncharacteristic tears.

Anyone would think she'd never encountered a hard luck story in her life; as it was her heart felt as if an iron fist were slowly squeezing the life from it. What was it about this man that turned her all squidgy and sentimental…and, yes, *protective*? He was big and bold enough to get by without her misplaced maternal instincts. But then there was nothing remotely maternal about the way Josh Prentice made her feel, she acknowledged unwillingly.

'How is Liam?'

'Asleep, I hope. As we all should be…I'm on the rosta for milking in the morning, which according to my watch isn't very long away…'

Flora noticed for the first time the faint bluish smudges under his eyes. 'Early mornings like that would kill me.'

'I got used to "Liam" hours some time ago and I've never needed much sleep, although I must admit…' He glanced once more at his watch.

His restlessness suddenly made sense; he wanted to be going and he hadn't bargained on a lovesick female giving him career advice in the wee hours. She was being incredibly thick—the man had chosen to sacrifice his sleep in order to avoid her. That did kind of hint that he didn't want her company.

'You want paying…of course. Will a cheque do?' She froze; her entire nervous system went into shock mode. Her eyes slowly widened in horror. *Lovesick!* Of course! It's taken you long enough! a small mocking voice in her skull informed her.

'Is anything wrong?'

Flora forced her mouth into a stiff smile. She shook her head. 'No, nothing.' If you discounted discovering you'd fallen in love for the first time. 'I just thought for a minute I'd lost my handbag, but I left it downstairs.' His cue to precede her down the narrow stairs—frustratingly he didn't move. 'Will a cheque do?'

'Cheque...?' Sleep deprivation seemed to be fuddling his normal mental dexterity. His eyes were moving in a distracted manner over her tense figure.

'You've finished the job,' she pointed out.

'I don't want your money,' he announced in a bewilderingly belligerent manner.

'What? Oh, it's not my money really,' she assured him earnestly. 'Claire will reimburse me.' Actually she'd decided the nursery make-over would be a nice thank-you for her friend, who had come up with the offer of this convenient bolt-hole in her hour of need.

His jawline still stayed steely and inflexible despite her assurances. 'No.'

Flora's exasperation reached new heights. When she thought of all the nice, *easy*, manageable men she might have fallen for she could have wept. No, *I* had to fall for this stupid, stubborn, incomprehensible man who doesn't even like me! Nice one, Flora!

'What's your problem?' she enquired spikily.

'I don't have a problem. I enjoyed doing this...' His expansive gesture took in the entire room. 'It was therapeutic.'

Flora wasn't sure she believed this unlikely claim. Therapy implied relaxation and he didn't look like a man who was relaxed; in fact he looked almost as strung out as she felt.

'Well, some people might think getting paid for something you enjoy is what it's all about. I enjoy what I do, but I have no problem with the pay cheque at the end of the month.'

'Shall we just call it the start of a whole new career and leave it at that?'

Tears of frustration formed in her eyes and she blinked them back. 'No, we won't!' she cried, bringing her shoe-less foot down hard on the boarded floor. 'Silly, misplaced pride won't buy Liam new shoes,' she reminded him angrily. 'It's not charity, you earned it...' she glanced in the direction of his handwork '...and more.'

'I'm not taking money off you, so the subject's closed.'

'You're so obstinate!' she breathed. 'But I can't accept your generosity, it's not...not appropriate.'

'I'm not being generous!' he growled. One angry, spontaneous stride brought him to her side.

They stood chin to chin or, rather, chin to chest; Flora lifted her head to rectify this situation. His physical presence, the sheer magnetism of the man was the most exciting and intimidating thing she'd encountered in her life. She felt burningly hot and teeth-chatteringly cold simultaneously, a situation which probably broke all known laws of science, but then the way she felt about him broke all laws of logic so why not? Giddily she met his seething grey eyes; they were filled with a depth of smouldering anger that she couldn't understand.

'Do you really want to know what I'm like?' His deep voice reverberated with disgust. His chest was heaving as he drew in air in great gulping breaths. *'Shall I tell you...?'* he challenged.

Flora didn't respond—she couldn't. His grip on her shoulders made her wince, but it was the only thing keeping her upright and had been since her knees had responded to the musky masculine scent of him and stopped offering her shaking body any support at all.

The sound of the phone sliced through the stark silence that followed. Josh's eyes went automatically to the mobile clipped on his belt.

'It must be mine, I left it downstairs.'

'Are you going to answer it?' he asked tersely.

'I should…' she admitted quietly. The anticlimax was extreme.

He stood to one side and she shot past him.

At some point during the conversation he had come into the room; Flora wasn't sure when that was. She looked up in surprise when he came over and took the dead phone from her limp grasp.

'What's happened?' His eyes assessed her blank, bruised-looking expression.

'My father's dead,' Flora explained, her brow furrowing in confusion because he couldn't be…how could he be? 'It happened this evening; he had a heart attack.' She raised her eyes to his face. 'Isn't this the part where you say you're very sorry?' The numbness was complete; it encased her like a strait-jacket of ice.

Josh didn't express his sorrow, but his eyes were warmly compassionate. He'd stopped confusing what he felt for the father with what he felt for the daughter. In fact he'd already come to the conclusion that he couldn't destroy the father if that meant hurting this young woman. Which meant what…? Josh thought he knew, but he wasn't ready yet to face the answer.

'Sit down,' he suggested.

She shook her head and began to pace the room, lifting a distracted hand to her blonde head every so often. 'He'd lost everything, his status, his job. They weren't going to strike him off the register, but he'd lost the respect and trust of his patients so what was the point carrying on?

That's what he said,' she told him dully. 'What's that?' she mumbled as he thrust a glass into her hand.

'Brandy.'

'It's Claire's.'

'I don't think she'll mind,' he encouraged softly.

Flora screwed up her nose and shuddered as the alcohol hit her taste buds, but dutifully she swallowed.

'Apparently it started in a pretty benign sort of way after my mother died.' Her eyes were closed when she spoke. 'Tranquillisers, that sort of thing.' Josh didn't think she was even talking to him in particular—she was just talking.

'I don't think he even realised he was hooked, but she did, the new secretary.' She lifted bitter blue eyes to his face. 'She tried to blackmail him into supplying her and her friends with drugs. He said that was when he realised how low he'd sunk.' Angrily she brushed the tears from her face. 'He went to the police and confessed, only she had been there before him. She was determined to take him down with her, you see. The court threw out the charges because there wasn't enough proof. Of course there wasn't enough proof—Dad wasn't a drug dealer, he was a sad, lonely man!' she cried. 'The damage had been done though; the press had latched onto the story.'

Her eyes suddenly opened; they blazed with self-condemnation. 'If I'd spent less time building up my career and more... If I'd been there when he needed me...it wouldn't...! He was lost without Mum. I don't ever want to do that,' she told him wildly, 'love someone so much I can't function without them.' She gave a wild hiccough. 'At least there wouldn't have been a chance of that with Paul.' Her face crumbled as the tears began to fall in earnest.

Josh took the glass from her hand before it was dropped to the floor and pushed her down into a convenient chair.

He laid a soothing hand to the back of her head and drew it towards him.

Flora stayed with her head pressed against his stomach, her arms looped around his waist, until the violent outburst abated. Finally she lifted her head, sniffing and dabbing her blotchy face with the back of her hand.

'I'm sorry.'

'No need, my shoulder is well known for bawling purposes, or, in this case—' he pressed a hand to his flat midriff '—my belly.'

'I have to go back to London.'

Visibly the threads of her self-control knitted smoothly together. It was almost as though the distraught young woman of moments before had never existed, he marvelled. For the first time since he'd met her she bore some resemblance to the ice-cool woman who'd treated the media circus with mild contempt.

'You should get some rest first.'

She shook her head dismissively. 'I need to make...' Josh saw her throat muscles spasm '...I need to make arrangements, and I mean *need*,' she told him fiercely. If you were doing something practical you couldn't think— thinking was painful. She gave a brisk smile; she wanted to dispel any fears he might be harbouring that she was going to start leaning on him either physically or any other way!

'Well, you can't drive,' he announced flatly. She opened her mouth to deny this claim when he nodded significantly towards the open brandy bottle on the dresser.

'Hell!' She set her mouth determinedly. 'It'll have to be the train, then. I need a taxi to take me to Bangor.'

'I'll take you.'

'*You!*'

'Yes, me. You pack or whatever, and I'll let Geraint

know what's happening. The express doesn't leave until five-thirty,' he added, when she looked impatient enough to start walking if they didn't leave immediately.

'Are you sure?' she fretted.

'Absolutely.'

True to his word, Josh returned by the time she had flung a few personal items in an overnight bag. 'I could drive, you know,' she said as he led the way to his four-wheel drive. 'I only swallowed a mouthful.'

'You could also fall asleep at the wheel and cause an accident,' he informed her sternly.

Flora lapsed into silence as she could hardly deny this accusation. Josh didn't attempt to make conversation or cheer her up on the way to the station and she was glad to be left alone with her own thoughts.

Her father's death still didn't seem real; she'd only spoken to him last night on the telephone and for the first time since the court case he'd sounded almost optimistic about the future. As the conversation they'd had replayed in her head over and over pain lodged as a solid, inexpressible ache in her chest.

'The last thing I wanted to do was hurt you, Flora.' He'd returned to this theme several times. Nothing she'd said had been enough to ease his bitter self-recrimination.

Josh passed her her overnight bag as she stepped into the first-class carriage. 'I do know how you feel, you know, and it probably won't help me saying it, but it does get easier.'

Rigid with contemptuous anger, she rounded on him, but she bit her lip to hold back her snarling response as it hit her that he was speaking the truth—he *did* know how she was feeling. She ventured a small noncommittal nod.

'I didn't pay you for my ticket!' she exclaimed, recalling suddenly that she'd stood passively by whilst he'd paid her fare. She began scrabbling feverishly in her bag, knocking several items on the floor in the process. Tears of frustration began to form in her eyes and she angrily brushed them away. 'I can't find…'

'Forget it!' Arms folded across his chest, he stood there on the platform acting as if he had money to burn, and it was first class! She didn't know what she wanted to do most: strangle him or kiss him.

'Don't do this again!' she pleaded. 'It's a lovely, kind gesture but you can't pay for me, Josh, you don't have any…' She bit her tactless tongue.

'You can owe me,' he offered calmly, apparently not put out by her reference to his financial circumstances. 'Will you be coming back?' The question was casual, but the intense expression in his eyes suggested otherwise.

Flora's agitated efforts abruptly ceased as she squatted there on the carriage floor. Her heightened emotions told her that something momentous had just occurred.

'I…I…will you be here?' she wondered huskily.

Eyes still sealed with hers, he nodded slowly. 'I will if you want me to be.'

She gave a shuddering sigh; she instinctively knew that Josh wasn't a man to make promises lightly. 'I do want that,' she told him simply. She got shakily to her feet and gripped the edge of the open window.

Josh could see the tears in her eyes shimmering as the train drew out.

It was a little thing perhaps—Flora didn't know yet—but the knowledge that she'd be going back and he'd be there, waiting, somehow sustained her through the next few days. She didn't know how much she'd been longing to return until she arrived back at the cottage almost a week later in a state of feverish anticipation.

I'm probably making one hell of a fool of myself, she

mused wryly as she tramped along the footpath that led to the farm. All the logic and common sense in the world couldn't stop her heart racing in anticipation as the cluster of whitewashed buildings that composed Bryn Goleu came into view.

She was almost running when she came across Geraint, who was gently chastising a young dog in his native tongue.

'He's young and has a lot to learn, doesn't he, girl?' he said, switching to English as he rubbed the ears of the patient older dog beside him. 'You after Josh, then?'

I suppose I am! Boldly she nodded, refusing to be intimidated by the amused glow in the young man's eyes.

'You'll find him in the barn, *cariad*.' He gestured down the hill.

'Thanks.'

Already striding out across the rocky ground followed by the two dogs, he waved a casual backward hand in response to her gratitude.

The barn was dim and filled with the sweet, earthy scent of hay bales which were piled high all around. Flora saw Josh before he saw her. Stripped to the waist, his olive-toned skin gleamed with a fine sheen of sweat. As she watched he paused in his labours and slowly rotated his head, stretching the tight muscles in his neck and shoulders. She caught her breath sharply, covetously watching the play of lean, rippling muscle over firm smooth flesh.

Josh looked around instantly.

'Hello!' she mumbled stupidly.

'How was it?' he asked, his eyes greedily taking in every detail of her appearance.

A shadow passed over her face and her mouth quivered

as her rigid control momentarily slipped. 'Pretty terrible,' she confirmed huskily.

'When did you get back?'

'About fifteen minutes ago.' Her cheeks flamed. Why be coy, Flora? Just go ahead and tell him you were so pathetically desperate to see him you didn't even unpack the car! 'I'm disturbing you...'

'Always,' he confirmed huskily.

'Your work...'

'I was about to take a break, do you want to...?'

'*Yes, please!*' she rushed in quickly. 'Dear God!' she groaned, covering her blushes—the visible ones at least—with her hands. 'I don't believe I'm doing this!'

'What are you doing, Flora?'

The gap between her fingers widened and she peered out. 'It's very nice of you to act like you haven't noticed, but I'm acting like...I'm coming on to you like a hussy,' she told him with a very unhussy-like blush.

'A very beautiful hussy,' he qualified, gently peeling the last of her fingers away from her face. 'Welcome home, Flora.' His bold glance was warm and intimate as he locked her startled eyes to his so tight she couldn't even blink.

'Home,' she echoed thickly. Her body was screaming out in need.

'Isn't that where the heart is...?'

'I think it might be, Josh...?' A deep shudder ran through her body as the tension inside her reached a critical level.

'Come here,' he instructed, his voice rough velvet.

The dam inside her broke and she didn't need asking twice. She walked into his arms, which happened to open just at the right moment. His head lowered towards her and she sank her fingers possessively into his thick glossy

hair—she wasn't taking any chances; if he changed his
mind about the kiss she might go quietly bonkers. He
didn't change his mind.

Slowly her blue eyes flickered open and she made a
small sound of deep contentment as his head finally lifted.
In that moment her selective senses were only aware of
things which were directly connected with him—things
like the warm, musky male smell that came from his body,
the damp, satiny texture of his glorious skin, the impression of controlled strength in his embrace. She took in with
primitive pleasure all the things that were part and parcel
of this man she'd fallen in love with.

The hand which had rested on the slender curve of her
waist slid lower, testing the firm, taut curve of her bottom.
His exploration caused him to groan deeply. He pulled her
hard against him to show her the urgency of his desire and
his face contorted in a grimace that was almost agony as
he gazed with raw desire at her flushed face.

'This probably isn't too clever,' he admitted reluctantly.
'Someone might come in.'

Flora trailed a finger down his lean cheek and shivered
when he turned his head to kiss the tip. She ran the same
slightly damp finger along the sensual outline of his lips.

'Isn't that traditionally the girl's line?' she asked huskily.

'I don't think you're like any traditional girl I've ever
met.'

'Is that good?' she enquired softly, stretching up on tip-
toe to chew softly at his lower lip. She gave a sigh and
rubbed the tip of her nose against his. 'I adore your
mouth,' she told him without a shred of overstatement or
self-consciousness. 'It's utterly *utterly* perfect.' She scrutinised with hungry reverence the sternly sexy outline of
his lips.

'I wish all my critics were like you.'

'You got any problems, point them in my direction.'

His lips twitched as she made her throaty declaration of war. 'That's mighty generous of you, little lady,' he drawled.

She cleared her throat. 'I hate to spoil a beautiful moment...'

'It is, isn't it?' he agreed smugly. The lure of her luscious lips proved an irresistible temptation to Josh. He plunged headlong into all that sweet, soft taste of heaven.

A breathless Flora tenaciously rediscovered the thread of her complaint. 'But I do have a slight problem with the "little lady" thing.' In truth, the patronising term made her feel kind of small and delicate, as if he could pick her up and put her in his pocket in a nice, cherishing sort of way.

Then just as she was puzzling over this evidence of a hitherto unexpected character trait—a desire to feel cherished—Josh quite suddenly did pick her up. He didn't put her in his pocket though, just in a snug, sweet-smelling cavern tucked away amongst the hay bales.

Far more promising than a pocket, she decided as his hip nudged hers with delicious familiarity as he lay down beside her. Resting on one elbow, he brushed a few soft strands of bright hair from her face.

With a slow, languorous smile she stretched like a cat. 'This puts a whole new slant on a roll in the hay.' Despite the lightness of her words there was a raw throb of emotion in her voice as she gazed up at him.

'Forget rolling,' he advised thickly as he reached down to dextrously flick open the top button of her shirt. He paused a moment to admire the curve of her collar-bone and the creamy flawless perfection of her skin before moving on to the next button. 'Conserve your energy.'

Flora didn't think she had an energy problem; every time he touched her she generated enough electricity to power the national grid! He watched her small breasts rise and fall in their light, lacy covering as he finally pulled aside her shirt. The expression in his eyes robbed her of breath.

Her head had fallen to one side. When he pressed his thumb to the point of her chin her face fell bonelessly against his supportive hand. He could feel the heavy vibration of the pulse spot at the base of her lovely throat.

'Flora? Are you all right?' he asked, his voice rough with sudden concern. The concave hollow of her flat belly deepened as her ribcage rose and fell rapidly. Her waxy pallor began to alarm him.

Her eyes, deep, drenching blue eyes, flickered open and relief shot through him.

'Never felt better,' she assured him, putting her heart into each syllable.

'Perhaps this isn't a good idea,' he said slowly, doubt beginning to cloud his eyes. 'You've had a traumatic time…'

Flora reached up and, grabbing the back of his hair, yanked his head down. 'Not half as traumatic as you'll have if you try and weasel out of this!' she hissed. 'I'm in full possession of my wits. I know *exactly* what I'm doing!' she told him fiercely.

Josh grinned, his teeth flashing white in his tanned face. 'I'll come quietly,' he promised, holding up his hands in mock surrender. 'Ouch!' He winced as several strands of hair came away in her fingers.

Flora examined the dark strands wrapped around her fingers. 'Sorry.' She grimaced. She levered herself upright. 'It's not as if you haven't got plenty to spare,' she felt impelled to point out as she examined the lush crop of hair that still clung firmly to his head.

'Just now I'm not interested in my follicle count.'

'Really? Most men when they reach your age get very interested. Why, I know…*oh*!' she mouthed silently as he pressed her back down into the hay and covered her with his body. A nudge of his knee had her thighs parted to provide just enough space for him to fit his long legs in between.

'Isn't this cosy?' he purred, running an exploratory hand down as far as her quivering flank.

Not the first description that sprang to Flora's mind, but she wasn't in the mood to argue with him about anything whilst he carried on doing all these deliciously wicked things to her.

He kissed her and carried on kissing her until she forgot to breathe, forgot her own name…but not his…never his. His name was etched on her soul in letters a mile high, because she loved him. She'd never dreamt that submission could feel so wonderful.

She never could figure out how or when he'd removed her shirt and bra without her noticing. It was his ragged gasp and the direction of his stark, needy stare that eventually drew her attention to her nudity. Always at ease with her body, she experienced a fleeting moment's concern, so great was her need to please him. His next throaty words dispelled any fledgling doubts.

'I wanted you since the moment I saw you. I didn't know how much until now…' he rasped. 'You're incredible.'

He couldn't take his eyes off her. Her nipples were small, yet plump and pouting. And surprisingly dark against her creamy skin like sweet, ripe berries. Taking hold of each soft, firm mound expertly in his big hands, he bent his head to suckle first one and then, when he'd had his fill, the other.

Flora's back arched as she gave herself up totally to the sensual pleasure of his touch. He was curved over her, and his mouth moved from her tingling, aching breasts, up the vulnerable line of her graceful throat until he reached her tenderly swollen lips.

Fingers splayed, Flora let her hands glide over the broad, hair-roughened expanse of his chest down his washboard-flat belly. She felt him suck in his breath and saw the quiver of muscles beneath his smooth skin respond helplessly to her touch.

Breath coming in short, anguished gasps, her tongue firmly tucked between her teeth—nobody looked at her best drooling—she began to unbuckle the leather belt that was looped through the waistband of his washed-out denims. Her co-ordination was shot to hell!

The basic skill seemed to be beyond her clumsy capability. Sweating with effort, she suddenly gave a sharp cry of frustration and pulled hard until his braced knees collapsed and he was on top of her. Feeling ever so slightly frantic, she pressed herself against him, glorying in the hard impression of his erection against the softness of her lower belly.

'I want…I want,' she babbled brokenly.

'Hush, honey, I know,' he soothed with indulgent roughness. Displaying none of her incompetence, he swiftly divested her of her jeans and shoes. A wolfish grin eased the tension stamped on his face as he contemplated the final item, a tiny lacy scrap, before he let it drift to the ground.

'A natural blonde.'

She opened her mouth to remonstrate him for ever doubting it, but her vocal cords didn't respond.

The air felt cool on her overheated skin, but it did nothing to reduce her inner temperature, which continued to boil. Her eyes felt heavy as she raised her slightly startled eyes from her own state of undress to Josh.

He had stood up to slide his jeans, closely followed by his boxer shorts, over his narrow hips. Inhibition was obviously a term he didn't understand. He made an intimidatingly erotic picture as he stood there naked, and obviously...*very* obviously aroused.

'Don't just stand there, man!' Her words started as an imperious command and ended as a desperate breathy plea. That was exactly how Flora felt: desperate and totally out of control.

Just watching him move turned her insides hotly molten. He touched her body; his hands and lips seemed to know exactly how to drive her sweetly out of her mind. She cried out in feeble hoarse protest as he located her most sensitive area and was relieved when Josh ignored her. As the moisture from his marauding mouth evaporated it left burning trails over her flesh.

'So wet for me,' he moaned brokenly, lifting his head.

Kneeling between her thighs, Josh cupped her bottom in his hands. Eyes like molten metal melded with hers, he thrust himself with agonising slowness into her, and the intensity of the febrile tremors which shook her body intensified even further. The breath fled her lungs in a series of fluttering gasps as he filled her.

Josh felt the tight, delicious resistance of her body as he obeyed the elemental compulsion to thrust deeper into her slick, receptive heat.

'Dear sweet...' An almost feral groan was wrenched from his dry throat as her ankles locked in the small of his back.

She hadn't known *wanting* could be like this. Nothing

in her life had prepared her for the raw intensity of this
degree of sheer *feeling*. Every nerve in her body was
screeching for a gratification she suddenly felt sure existed,
she just wasn't sure how it happened. The idea of not
fulfilling the expectation that held every muscle in her
body rigid made her frantic.

'Yes, oh, yes, I want all of you, Josh…' She sobbed as
her fingers clutched at the distended corded muscles of his
shoulders and forearms.

Josh responded with fervour to her plea. Delirious with
delight, Flora matched his rhythm move for move as the
intensity of his measured strokes grew increasingly frenzied, increasingly desperate. She cried out in startled pleasure as it hit her, her teeth closed over the damp skin of
his neck as a shocked hoarse cry emerged from her dry
throat.

'I didn't know!' She sobbed as she felt the last hot,
pulsing surges of his body within her before he stilled,
breathing hard.

His big, wonderfully sweat-slick body felt deliciously
heavy against her. One long leg remained looped over his
hip as he rolled to one side. She could feel his heart still
pounding hard. The situation was deliciously intimate, just
as much in a different way as their frenzied coupling of
moments before.

'It's never happened to me before, you see,' she explained in a distracted manner. 'If I'd married Paul it might
never have,' she realised, her eyes widening in horror in
her flushed face. No longer orgasmically uneducated, she
knew *exactly* what she'd been missing. 'That would have
been…'

'A terrible waste,' Josh completed softly. He tucked a
stray damp strand of hair behind her ear before running a

gentle hand down the soft contour of her cheek. His eyes were quite extraordinarily tender.

Paul the prat had certainly earned his name, he thought scornfully. Before Bridie he'd had a series of casual liaisons which he was neither ashamed nor proud of, but even though the emotions involved on both sides had been shallow he had got as much satisfaction from providing his partner with pleasure as taking it himself. When he'd eventually fallen in love, adding an emotional element to the equation had only intensified this need to give pleasure and he felt deeply scornful of men who missed out on this enjoyment.

His response made Flora blush—how could you blush with a man you'd just done *that* with? It probably was quite terribly bad taste to discuss a previous lover with your current lover, she pondered worriedly. She didn't want Josh to think she was the sort of girl who went around bitching about male inadequacies—not that he had any! Flora found she didn't like thinking even briefly about a day when Josh would be an ex.

'Never?' he persisted, a note of incredulity entering his deep voice. She showed an inclination to bury her face in his shoulder but a finger under her chin wouldn't permit this cowardly retreat.

'I guess I've been doing something wrong...?' she mumbled.

'Not so that I noticed,' he responded warmly. 'You know what this means, don't you...?' A small worried frown pleated her smooth forehead. 'It means you have a lot of time to make up,' he explained cheerfully. 'But don't worry—I'm prepared to put some overtime in on the job if you are.' He gently extracted several odd stalks of hay from her hair.

Flora smiled slowly. She was, she definitely was! This

hadn't felt like a one-night stand, but it was good to hear him say something to confirm this.

'Unfortunately, now probably isn't the best time to start. Megan produces afternoon tea about this time and if I'm not there she'll probably come looking.'

'Oh!' Flora gasped, glancing down at their intertwined naked bodies, and realised it might prove a bit embarrassing if they were discovered like this. A bit was probably a massive understatement! The fact she had made love in a barn in the middle of the afternoon was growing more extraordinary with each passing second—talk about out of character! But then, she mused, reflecting thoughtfully on the dramatic contrast between shockingly aggressive aspects of her behaviour during their love-making and the compulsive need to relinquish control...surrender to him...maybe she was just getting acquainted with parts of her character which had been submerged.

She watched from under the protective sweep of her lashes as Josh got lithely to his feet. He really was awesome. Maybe the answer was even simpler—she'd just not met Josh Prentice before!

It took her longer than it should to dress because Josh, who'd donned his clothes almost as fast as he'd shed them, stood there watching every move she made. Consequently every move she made was incredibly clumsy.

'Do you want to join me for tea? Megan would love to meet you, Liam still remembers his ''smelly lady''—you made quite an impression...'

'On Liam...?' she enquired, shamelessly fishing.

'On us both,' he remarked, a somewhat grim expression flickering across his face. 'We could go out to dinner tonight if you'd like? Somewhere we can talk.'

'A date?'

A date, dear God, Josh, what the hell are you doing?

What was he thinking? Hell, he'd already done it! 'Yes, a date,' he confirmed recklessly.

So much for not going anywhere with this until he'd explained the situation! Problem was he hadn't been thinking with his head when he'd turned around and seen her staring at him—staring at him with those big, hungry 'kiss me' eyes. All the prepared explanations had vanished on the spot. How did you go about explaining to a woman that the original motivation for seducing her had been revenge? Candlelight and a romantic atmosphere—not to mention a lot of wine—might make the task easier, but somehow he doubted it.

'I could cook if you like, it might be more...' she coloured prettily '...private.' She really liked the idea of having him to herself but she was also worried about the state of his bank balance. She didn't want him to feel obliged to make an extravagant gesture. 'Claire left the freezer crammed with food and *she's* a very good cook.'

'That would be good.' A public place might not be a good idea if she started throwing things when he told her.

CHAPTER FIVE

'It's instinct, you know.'

Josh squinted against the glare of the sun as he emerged from the barn. A man moved out from the shadows of the outbuilding closely followed by a Border collie who growled warningly at the intruder.

'Nice boy,' the stranger said as he nervously edged away from the dog.

Josh called the animal to his side with a click of his fingers. 'What can I do for you?'

The stranger gave a grin and rocked cockily on the balls of his feet. 'You don't remember me, do you?'

'Actually I do,' Josh contradicted.

The grin wilted but he made a swift recovery. 'Came to you straight like a little homing pigeon, didn't she?' His lascivious leer brought Josh's temper to simmering point in a heartbeat.

Where was his telephoto when he needed it? the journalist wondered, blissfully unaware of the homicidal stirrings seething in the younger man's breast. He was pretty sure that whatever had been going on in that barn would have made very good copy.

'I've not lost the old gut instinct,' he congratulated himself out loud.

'Or the gut,' Josh drawled unkindly.

Tom Channing automatically sucked in the belly which spilled gently over his belt. He smiled tightly; he could afford to be generous. 'No need to be nasty, Mr Prentice. Does she know?'

'Was that meant to take me off guard?' Josh enquired in a mildly bored voice.

'Then she doesn't.' The journalist smirked triumphantly. 'I knew I'd seen your face somewhere before, I'm good with faces. Then it came to me—you were that artist bloke they all rave about. On the off chance I looked up your bio and up popped the stuff about your wife snuffing it, and lo and behold her surgeon just happened to be Sir David Graham...you know, I don't believe in coincidence.'

'You know,' Josh commented languidly, 'I guessed you didn't.'

'You were following her too, weren't you, that day?'

'This is your story.' Josh's casual gesture invited the journalist to continue.

'I don't know what your game is exactly, but I can guess.' His smirk made Josh wonder how long he would be able to stop himself rearranging those sickeningly smug features. 'Have you thought how much more satisfying your little vendetta would be if it became public knowledge?' He paused to let the idea sink in. 'How I slept with the daughter of my wife's killer. How do you like that?'

'A little ambitious syllable-wise for the sort of newspaper you work for, isn't it? It is the *Clarion*, isn't it?'

'How do you know that?' With a puzzled frown the thickset man produced a rolled-up tabloid sheet from his pocket and proudly displayed the lurid headline to Josh. 'One of mine.' He gave a philosophical shrug when the artist type remained stubbornly unawed. 'Partners...?'

Josh's lip curled as he looked at the extended hand and his face hardened. Tom Channing realised for the first time that the big guy wasn't going to play the game; his friendly air faded abruptly leaving the older man looking just plain mean and spiteful.

'Well, it's up to you,' the journalist told him in an off-hand manner. 'I'll write it with or without your help,' he warned.

'Tell me, do you like your job?'

Tom was beginning to feel a bit edgy. He could predict the way people acted in this situation and this guy wasn't doing any of the predictable things. He didn't look angry or panicked. He just wasn't acting the way people did when they realised he held all the cards.

'Sure I do.' And truth to tell, with his track record with the bottle and a couple of minor disasters that had occurred before he'd dried out the last time, he was lucky he had it, because no other national was going to look twice at him these days. What he needed was a really big story: *this* story!

'And of course you were really lucky when they didn't sack you after the Manchester debacle, weren't you? It probably helped that the editor back then was an old drinking buddy from way back—though he's retired now, hasn't he? Tell me, how do you get on with the new broom?'

'How do you know about Manchester?' There was a slight tremor in the hack's hand as he wiped away the sweat from his gleaming forehead with the cuff of his shirt.

'You're not the only one who can do a bit of research, and I have to tell you mine was more thorough than yours. I wanted to know what sort of man gets turned on by scaring a woman, and I found out.'

A dark flush travelled up the older man's thick neck. 'She wasn't scared!' he protested.

'Just as your ex wasn't when you put her in hospital the last time.'

The blustering journalist coloured unattractively.

'If Flora Graham had been scared she wouldn't have

shown it.' An admiring light flickered briefly in Josh's grey eyes.

'All this moral outrage is rich coming from you!' Tom Channing sneeringly hit back. 'She was a hell of a lot safer with me than she is with you. My motives are positively *pure* by comparison!'

Josh's nostrils flared as his mouth compressed into a savage white-rimmed line. 'If you want to keep your job,' he advised grimly, 'forget you ever met Flora Graham, forget you even know her name. The only reason you want to hurt her,' he continued in a soft, controlled voice that really shook Tom—shook him almost as much as the ferocious expression in those spooky pale eyes, 'is that she is untainted by the sordid world you live in. You hate it because you can't bring her down to your level, because she's simply a fine human being.'

'My, you've *really* fallen for her!' Mentally he was rewriting those headlines; this got better and better, he decided gleefully. His grin faded dramatically as Josh's fists clenched. This was not your typical effete arty type he was dealing with, he reminded himself. This guy might be greyhound lean but he gave the impression he could cause serious damage if he wanted—and right now he looked as if he wanted! Time to leave...he had his story.

'Got a phone on you?'

The journalist blinked at the unexpected question.

'Of course you have. Got your boss's number?'

'Listen, friend, there's no point you bleating to Jack Baker. He won't...'

'I don't mean your new editor, I mean the proprietor, David Macleod, the bloke who owns the whole stinking rag. Ring David and tell him you want to write this story, then tell him Josh Prentice isn't happy.' Under the circumstances he felt no qualms about employing a little judicious blackmail; to protect Flora he'd go a hell of a lot further.

'You're bluffing.' He stared incredulously at the stony-faced guy in front of him. 'There's no way you could have that much clout.' A shade of uncertainty had entered his voice.

'You of all people should know that money talks and I have serious money,' Josh explained casually. 'And good friends. There was a time when David needed some financial backing and I like to help my friends out... You see, your bio on me left out a few very important details, like I made my first million before I was twenty-one.'

Tom Channing went pale. 'You're having me on!'

Josh shrugged. 'Take the risk,' he suggested generously. 'I don't give a damn, but let me tell you one thing—you print a single derogatory syllable about Flora Graham and I'll take you apart slowly, piece by piece.'

Tom Channing saw no reason to disbelieve him. It seemed to him that the prospect of this dismemberment seemed to make Prentice very happy. This guy, he decided, was an animal and that contrast of the friendly voice and that Grim Reaper glare really chilled his marrow good and proper!

'Freedom of the press...' he objected weakly.

Josh snorted derisively. 'Principles from you! You sold out any principles you had twenty years back and we both know it. And please don't give me that ''the public have a right to know'' bull, or I'll crack up!' Josh snarled, showing no immediate inclination to laugh. 'There's no national interest involved here. There's just a vindictive little has-been hack, inventing lurid details to do a hatchet job on someone who's never done anyone any harm! Try selling this one on the open market and I'll be forced to reveal how I saw you assaulting Miss Graham after you'd followed her to a lonely secluded spot.'

'I hardly touched her...' The journalist protested as he saw plan B slip down the toilet.

'You *did* touch her though, and she didn't like it; that's enough to constitute an assault. You're not the only one who can be economical with the truth,' he admitted ruthlessly. 'Her father's dead, the story's dead. Do yourself a favour and stop working on your headlines.'

'I don't need to work on them, fact is one hell of a lot more entertaining than anything I could dream up here, mate.' The journalist choked.

Josh's lip curled. 'I'm not your *mate*.'

There came a time when a man had to cut his losses and make an exit with as much dignity as possible—in this case that wasn't very much! Tom automatically reached for the packet of cigarettes that lived in his breast pocket. His scowl deepened when he came up empty. He rolled back his sleeve and ripped off the nicotine patch with an expression of loathing. He'd quit next week.

'You haven't heard the last of me!' he yelled back over his shoulder.

The threat didn't bother Josh but the element of truth in some of the sleaze's jibes had. Soberly he made his way towards the farmhouse.

Josh knew the instant the cottage door closed behind him that something was seriously up. Flora stalked back into the small sitting room, without saying anything to him. Her slender back was screaming rejection. He glanced at the flowers in his hand expecting to see the blooms withered on their stems—it had been that sort of look she'd given him and his gifts. He placed the champagne and the flowers on the dresser.

'Sure you could *afford* them?' she snapped sarcastically as he entered close on her heels.

There was a faint tremor in her fingers as she picked up and replaced with exaggerated care a pretty gingerpot decorated with a traditional blue and white design. It was incredibly hard to control her destructive impulses. When she thought about how he'd deliberately misled her she wanted to break things—preferably parts of his highly luscious body!

She shot him a sideways glance of loathing and saw with growing resentment that the luscious part was still disturbingly applicable. Black suited him, she concluded, taking in the tailored black trousers that suggested the muscularity of his thighs. If she hadn't discovered what a lying rat he was she'd probably already have unbuttoned that crisp cotton shirt to reveal...she closed her eyes and swallowed convulsively.

Josh closed his eyes too; knowing he deserved whatever was coming didn't make this situation any better. Dear God, he *had* to salvage something out of this mess. 'I meant to tell you earlier, Flora, but I...'

'Were having too good a laugh at my expense?' she suggested, placing a hand on one slender hip and thrusting the other out.

He doubted she even suspected how sexually provocative he found the pose...he wished he had his sketch-book with him...but then drawing things had always been his way of delaying the inevitable. After Bridie's death he'd painted himself into the ground before he'd stopped still long enough to let the grieving process kick in, and then he hadn't touched a paintbrush for a long time.

'You must have thought it *very* amusing when I offered you career advice. *Have you ever thought of painting?*' she cruelly caricatured her own starry-eyed enthusiasm. At the back of the drawer were a pile of prospectuses from various art colleges. She supposed she ought to be grateful she hadn't given him those yet!

With a dry-eyed sob of disgust she flung the incriminating colour supplement at him with such vigour the staples gave way and sheets of glossy paper scattered around the room.

'Although, compared to some of these critics, my admiration was pretty tepid!'

'You've found out what I do?' he said blankly, picking up a torn sheet of paper that bore a reproduction of one of his earliest efforts. Impatiently he screwed up the paper and dropped it on the floor.

Flora folded her arms and pursed her lips. 'Why, how many other secrets do you have?' She held up her hands. 'Don't tell me,' she pleaded contemptuously. 'I already know too much about you. You're nothing but a cheap fake…! Though maybe not that cheap, it seems your paintings go for a small fortune!' She made this sound like the worst insult of all.

A thin, ironic smile curved Josh's lips. 'It's not my artistic ability you object to, then, just the fact I'm not starving in some rat-infested attic!'

How dare he make it sound as if *I'm* the one being unreasonable? He couldn't begin to imagine how stupid and humiliated she'd felt when she'd realised who and what he was. It had all been a game for him. Had he ever been going to tell her? she wondered.

'I don't care if you're a bloody millionaire! I'm glad you find this funny!' She sniffed, furiously blinking away the tears of self-pity that stung her eyelids. Her determination to treat him with bland indifference had been long forgotten; in fact she'd forgotten it as the first pang of longing had hit, about the same instant he'd walked through her door. 'The thing I object to—' she choked as abject pity squirmed horridly in her stomach '—is being laughed at and lied to.'

'Did you let me make love to you because you thought I was a penniless decorator?' One darkly delineated brow rose enquiringly. 'Or were you just sorry for me, perhaps?' he suggested thoughtfully.

'Of course not, no, no on both accounts!' she hissed, outraged that he could even suggest such a thing. 'I did that because...' *No!* Under the circumstances that explanation was better left unsaid; she'd had a gut full of humiliation for one day! To her intense relief no sarky prompt was forthcoming.

'Then why does what I do for a living make a difference one way or the other?' he asked instead with infuriating logic.

'It's not what you do for a living, it's what you do by way of amusement which makes you a ratbag first class!' she informed him with lofty disdain. 'You lie...why, you do it so well, you could lie for Britain!' Her voice rose shrilly in volume as her contempt mounted. 'As liars go, Josh, you are world class! And I'm a world-class sap for falling for it. Do you always adopt a fake personality when you're away from home? Does it make it more difficult for your little local conquests to pursue you when you leave?'

'You're not a local,' he pointed out, watching with some fascination the undulations of her heaving, unfettered bosom. It seemed that at some point this evening she'd dressed to please someone—in all probability him—in a discreetly slinky misty blue number that clung in all the right places. 'And if you want to pursue me I'll draw you a detailed map; better still,' he offered extravagantly, 'I'll drive you myself.'

Flora's rapid breathing slowed a little. He sounded flatteringly sincere, but then he did sincere awfully well, she reminded herself.

'As for conquests, you and I both know that I hadn't slept with anyone for a very long time.'

Flora felt the colour fade from her overheated cheeks. She suddenly found it impossible to maintain eye contact... 'I'm no expert,' she gritted. In fact he must now know that compared to his her sexual repertoire was strictly limited. The sizzling spectre of his raw hunger rose up to add to her wretched confusion. He introduced the subject deliberately to confuse me, she concluded with irrational resentment.

'*You know,*' he contradicted confidently. 'Do you think you could give me a minute without throwing something at me or screaming abuse?'

If he thought this was abuse he'd led a very sheltered life! 'Miracles do happen,' she told him nastily. 'Even to the undeserving.'

'If you recall, I didn't say I was a decorator...did I?'

Flora's disgruntled sniff acknowledged this. 'But you didn't disillusion me!' Which in her book amounted to the same thing.

'True, but round about the time I should have straightened things out you'd just invited me into your home, Flora, and I wanted an excuse to be there—any excuse.' The look of stark hunger that flickered over his handsome face was too rawly genuine to be faked.

Flora caught her breath and blinked, the anger abruptly fled her body and, call her criminally susceptible, but the feelings that eagerly rushed in to fill the vacuum were dreamily sensuous.

'You did?' she whispered huskily.

He nodded and his lips quivered to form a faint wry

smile. 'Not that I admitted why I wanted to be there to myself at the time.' His confession held a savage inflection.

'No…?' She tried to stiffen her weakening resolve and fan the flames of her fury. 'What are you doing milking cows anyhow?'

'My brother is married to Nia, Geraint's sister. That makes me family…sort of. I was up here—' he paused slightly '—visiting.' Flora was too interested in discovering how he came to be acting as farm labourer in the middle of nowhere to notice the odd, almost belligerent inflection in his voice as he offered up the explanation for his presence on the farm.

'Huw, Geraint's dad, broke his leg, which makes them one man short at one of the busiest times of the year. I offered to extend my stay and help out a bit…mind you, I didn't intend to stay this long…'

'You didn't…?' It was hard not to sound smugly pleased.

He shook his head. 'Are you still mad with me, Flora?' he asked with a cajoling smile.

'I suppose you think that grin will get you everywhere.'

'It's worked so far.'

'I just bet it has,' she growled sourly. 'Well, you'll find I'm not such a pushover.' If only! Josh appeared to accept her strictures meekly—too meekly probably, she concluded suspiciously.

'I offered to cook for you because I thought you couldn't afford to take me out, and I didn't want to injure your masculine pride by offering to pay.'

'I know,' he admitted frankly. 'It made me feel like one hell of a heel.'

She sniffed; his remorse was a bit late coming. 'Not enough of a heel to tell me the truth,' she observed acidly.

'I *hate* cooking,' she added so that he'd appreciate the enormity of her sacrifice. 'I've thawed enough to feed an army.'

She'd read the article before she'd started preparing the meal so at that precise moment all the thawed food was dripping on the kitchen table. There must be some deep-buried sex-linked gene, she mused, that had suddenly made her feel she had to feed her man. Well, he wasn't hers in any strictly technical sense, but, she admitted to herself with a rush of honesty, she'd like it if he were! Such proprietorial instincts were alien to her; everything tonight was conspiring to unsettle her.

'It'll all ruin now,' she fretted.

'I'm not fussed about eating.'

'Aren't you hungry? All that physical labour mending…things…' Her technical knowledge of farming was seriously limited.

'The most physical thing I did today left me feeling amazingly invigorated,' he explained glibly.

If Flora had needed further elaboration the bold, bad gleam in his eyes was enough to confirm her initial suspicions.

'Me too,' she asserted huskily.

'I make a mean omelette, we could eat later…?' His deep, throaty voice trailed suggestively away. His burning eyes ignited a fire all of her own; it was inside—deep inside.

She shrugged. 'I suppose,' she conceded gruffly, 'that might be all right.'

'How all right?' he persisted.

Flora gave a disgruntled grunt of irritation and glared at him. 'All right,' she informed him spikily. 'It would be *very* all right. In fact, if you must know, it would be a hell of a lot more than all right, and in case you didn't get the drift I can't stand omelettes,' she added on the one-in-a-million chance he still had any doubts about what part of the evening's timetable she found attractive!

Josh's startled, delighted laugh was a low, sexy rumble that made her toes curl. 'My repertoire extends beyond omelettes.'

Just thinking about Josh's no doubt extensive repertoire made her stomach muscles cramp. A troubled light entered Flora's blue eyes. 'Mine's a bit limited,' she confessed; they both knew she wasn't talking culinary skills.

The memory of Paul's spiteful accusation was draining her confidence reserves—it wasn't as if she'd actually believed him at the time, not really... What made her think she could please a man? Especially one like Josh. Maybe Paul had been right—maybe she was frigid! She hadn't felt very frigid in Josh's arms; in fact she hadn't acted frigid either. The memory of how she'd acted brought a blast of colour to her cheekbones. Flora didn't look at him but she could feel Josh staring at her.

A firm hand on the angle of her jaw forced her reluctant head up. 'I don't have a little book filled with set game play, Flora.'

'I'm sorry,' she mumbled, embarrassed by her obvious plea for reassurance. She shook her head and missed the heavy swish of long hair; it had always distracted attention from her face very satisfactorily. Right now she needed some help with distractions; she felt wretchedly exposed. 'I'm not usually so *needy*.'

His eyes darkened. 'Me neither,' he told her throatily.

Flora's eyes grew round and a startled, 'Oh!' escaped her parted lips.

'You don't always have to stay in control of a situation,' he insisted.

'I think I do. Maybe I don't trust...'

He stiffened and she rushed in to mend any damage her careless comments had done.

'Not you, I don't distrust you.' She was so anxious to reassure him. 'It's me...I don't trust feeling this way. People do crazy things when they let...lust get out of hand...'

'*Lust.* I suppose that could be considered progress,' he murmured drily.

Flora was bewildered by the spark of anger in his eyes. 'I mean, think of what we did this afternoon...' she began worriedly.

'I am.'

An inarticulate moan escaped her lips. 'Funny man, you slay me,' she croaked. The irony was he did just that! 'Haven't you realised we didn't use...? I'm not taking the pill, you know...the contraceptive pill, that is,' she elaborated stiffly. 'I don't think there's *too much* danger of anything happening.' Her frown deepened. 'But that's not really the point...'

'It's very much the point,' he contradicted harshly. 'By "anything" I'm assuming you mean pregnancy?'

Flora nodded uncomfortably. 'I'm not really ready to get pregnant.'

'I'm not ready for you to be pregnant—*ever*,' he ground out white-faced and grim. His vehemence shouldn't have hurt her—it was only natural a man didn't want a child from a casual liaison—but it did! The sheer depth of his anger confused and wounded her.

'It wasn't just me being foolish and reckless,' she reminded him bitterly. You could mess around with euphemisms like spontaneous, but when you came down to it she'd been plain stupid and his reaction was only underlining her stupidity.

'Do you think I don't know that?' The lines bracketing

his strong mouth deepened. 'I wouldn't deliberately expose anyone I cared about to that sort of danger...' he grated. 'It was criminally irresponsible of me.' He ran a hand savagely through his hair and glared broodingly—seemingly blindly—ahead. 'As it was I took advantage of the fact you've been through a hellish time and you were screaming out for comfort...'

'I'm not a child, Josh. I knew *exactly* what I was doing,' she contradicted him firmly. 'And I wanted to do it. In fact,' she added, not much caring if she sounded brazen, 'I'd been imagining doing it since I met you, so it had nothing whatever to do with being grief-stricken.' She heard the sibilant hiss of his sharply indrawn breath. 'So if you feel the urge to don sackcloth and ashes leave my emotional traumas out of it,' she gritted stubbornly.

Suddenly it clicked: his wife had died in childbirth— small wonder he looked spooked at the idea of unplanned pregnancy. Poor Josh, it was *his* emotional traumas they were talking about here.

'Crossing the road is a calculated risk, Josh,' she reminded him gently. He looked down at her slim fingers against the dark cloth of his sleeve but he didn't reject her touch. 'I know that statistics don't mean anything when someone you love is the rare exception, but childbirth really isn't normally that dangerous these days.' Her eyelashes fluttered against her cheek as she blinked rapidly before raising stunned eyes to his face. 'Did you just say you cared about me?' she queried sharply.

He looked pretty overwhelmed by her abrupt query, or maybe it was her blatant admission that she'd been silently lusting after him since they'd met—looking the way he did you'd have thought he'd have been used to lecherous females. The dark bands of colour that stained the sharp crest of his cheekbones might even have indicated embarrassment, but at least he didn't avoid her eyes. He returned her scrutiny gravely and to her amazement made no effort to deny it or shrug her comment off as a joke.

'If I did, would that be saying too much, too soon?' There was an aggressive edge to his defensive query.

Was he kidding? Swallowing the solid lump of emotion that welled in her throat, she shook her head vigorously.

'Then I admit that I care for you—I care for you too much to gratify the urgings of your body clock. I think we should get one thing straight from the outset: if you want children from a relationship, I'm not your man,' he warned her heavily. 'I already have a child, you don't—so you could call it unfair.' His broad shoulders lifted and a thin, bitter smile formed on his lips. 'It probably is, but that's the way it is. When Bridie died I wanted to blame someone, anyone.' His nostrils flared as he took a deep breath before plunging further into explanations he had no experience of giving.

'It's taken a long time, but I've finally accepted that it wasn't something anyone could have predicted or prevented. The luck factor, or bad luck factor you refer to, just makes it worse if anything. I'm simply not prepared to take that risk with someone's life again. Take it or leave it.'

In other words take him or leave him! Feeling the way she did there wasn't ever a possibility that cool choice was going to enter in her decision. Even though, deep down, she knew that having this man's babies would bring her deep fulfilment, it was the man she wanted.

Babies. Relationships…! That was all a major leap from love-making in a hay barn! She'd automatically assumed his feelings were less intense than her own—a bit of stereotyping; it seemed she was wrong with a vengeance! Her fuddled brain couldn't keep pace with what he was telling her...what he was revealing about his expectations.

'I've seen couples who can't have children,' he continued, showing her a stony, unlover-like countenance. 'Seen how the constant preoccupation with procreation can drive a wedge between them. It's possible that knowing you could have a baby but your partner doesn't want one could be even worse.'

'Josh, are you saying you see us together...long term?'

A look of intense exasperation swept across his face. 'Hell, woman, do you think I'd be telling you this if I didn't? I just want you to know what you'd be getting into.'

A sudden naughty grin chased the last lingering shadows from her face. 'Into bed with you, I hope,' she announced boldly.

Josh responded with an equally roguish grin. The amusement slowly faded from his eyes as he took her by the shoulders. 'You're quite sure you understand that my terms are not negotiable?' he asked her sternly. 'You're not harbouring any foolish idea that you'll be able to change my mind eventually.'

'No,' she lied earnestly. 'If I knew you *couldn't* have children I'd still want to be...' A sudden notion occurred to her. 'You haven't had the...? Have you?'

He gave a very masculine wince. 'Snip? No, call me squeamish...'

'Not at all,' she responded swiftly, trying to disguise her relief with a businesslike practicality. 'There are other less drastic and perfectly successful forms of preventing fatherhood.' Not to mention motherhood!

Surely when the healing process was complete he'd see that his attitude was an overreaction—understandable, but nevertheless overreaction. Right now all that mattered to her was that Josh cared for her and they could be together. Her heart was bursting with optimism. Tomorrow could take care of itself; she was going to take care of Josh.

'And I came well supplied with one of those, but I'm open to any alternative suggestions.'

'Yes, well,' she croaked, trying and failing spectacularly to match his relaxed attitude to all things intimate.

Thumbs either side of her jaw, he bent his head and let his nose gently nudge the side of hers. She felt dizzy as his warm breath whispered over her skin and her body reacted of its own accord to being close to him.

'I need you, Flora. I need you to kiss me.' The ragged tempo of his breathing deepened. 'I need to feel your hands on my body, I need to feel your body on my body, I need like hell to be inside you...' The intense melting sensation between her legs made her shift restlessly as Josh groaned deeply and lifted his head. She could see that the strain in his voice was reflected in the taut lines of his strong, vibrantly handsome face.

'Is that needy enough for you?' he enquired, his sardonic gaze sweeping over her.

'Oh, yes,' she breathed gustily. *'Definitely.'* She allowed her sultry gaze to move slowly over the intriguing contours of his face before reaching up and laying her fingers on the back of his firm, strong neck. 'I really want to kiss you too,' she confessed huskily.

'I'm all for following your instincts, angel. That was a very mysterious smile?'

'No mystery,' she assured him dreamily. 'I was just thinking I don't feel very angelic just now.' Her body was almost audibly thrumming with the slow throb of sexual arousal; it bathed her...drenched her. She wanted Josh to make love to her more than she wanted anything—including babies, she firmly told the cold voice of logic that lurked discreetly in the back of her mind.

Sinking her fingers deeper into the lush dark growth on the back of his head, she set about doing something about the kissing part. He co-operated fully with her design, fully enough to leave her an inarticulate, clinging mass of screaming nerve-endings and equally noisy hormones by the time the lengthy embrace ended.

'Oh, my!' she half sobbed. 'You kiss beautifully.' She closed her eyes; looking at him made her feel dizzy.

'You do everything beautifully.' He watched with a ferociously rapt expression the delicate fluttering of her closed blue-veined eyelids.

She felt warmly compliant as he picked her up. His splendid physique was not just for show—he was amazingly strong. He was amazing in many ways, she mused, tightening her grip around his neck.

'I think we'll do this properly in a bed this time. Up here?' He inclined his head towards the narrow staircase.

'I thought you did it properly last time.'

'True,' he conceded modestly. 'But I'm still removing hay from places hay was never meant to be, very uncomfortable. Not that it isn't a price I'm willing to pay...'

She nodded in eager agreement. 'I hate to point out a flaw in your plan,' she said as he approached the narrow staircase, 'but, as much as I like this mode of transport...' and she did very much '...I don't think this is strictly practical.'

'It's too narrow, isn't it?'

''Fraid so.'

Josh lowered her reluctantly to the ground. 'A man does his best to be spontaneous.' His eyes gleamed as he smoothed the wrinkles in her dress thoroughly with the flat of his hand. 'Actually,' he confided, 'not actually spontaneous in the strictest sense—I've been working all day on this scene where I kick open the bedroom door and throw you masterfully on the bed.' He dwelt with visible pleasure on the cherished image.

'It sounds good to me. But don't say die, all is not lost,' she told him solemnly, entering into the spirit of things. 'How about it if I get up the stairs under my own steam and take it from there pretending you carried me up?' Eyes sparkling, she looked expectantly up at him.

'That's what I like to hear—lateral thinking,' he approved.

'Right, then!' she enthused, not feeling in the mood to delay things. Hitching up the long skirt of her dress in one hand, she attacked the stairs two at a time, fairly flying up them. When he reached the top she was standing there with her arms open.

'What are you waiting for?' she asked pertly.

Josh's deep, delighted laugh rang out. 'To wake up?' he wondered wryly.

'Nightmare?'

'Dream, angel, the best dream ever,' he told her truthfully, and he'd do anything, including lie, to keep that dream alive.

CHAPTER SIX

CAN he still taste me? Flora wondered dreamily, running the tip of her tongue sensuously around the outline of her full lips. When she breathed deeply all she could smell was the scent rising from her own warm, sticky skin; it was an erotic, mind-blowing combination of sex and Josh.

When her eyes flickered open they were still a deep, aroused navy blue. Each and every individual muscle in her body was totally relaxed in sharp contrast to the knife-edge tension of moments before. Silently she sighed with voluptuous pleasure at the memories still fresh in her mind. His love-making had brought her to a pitch of indescribable anticipation that had scarcely been bearable.

Her anxiety had reached fever pitch when she'd thought that she might not be permitted the pleasure of driving him a little crazy too. Huskily she'd told him what she wanted to do and happily he hadn't been too shocked by wanton requests she would have blushed to recall had she not been transformed into a totally shameless hussy. It was strange that Josh was the only man with whom she could imagine shedding every inhibition.

Her satiated stomach muscles quivered when she visualised his face as her greedy fingers had closed over the hard, silky length of him. It had been his turn to plead when her caresses had grown more intimate.

'I wish I could stay the night,' Josh murmured beside her. He reached over to rub the end of her twitching nose affectionately with the tip of one finger.

Lying replete in the crook of his arm, Flora stretched

voluptuously and flipped over onto her stomach and propped herself up on her elbows to look at him. Josh's attention was immediately drawn to the gentle sway of her small breasts as they adapted to her new position.

'Do you have to go yet?' she coaxed, her full lower lip quivering as she tried to suppress a strange and unusual urge to pout prettily.

The thing was she just wasn't herself. Just looking at his superb lithe body made her feel and act like a sexually deprived fool with an IQ in single figures, and the crazy part was she didn't care. Crossing her legs at the ankle, she wriggled her toes in the air. The movement made her freshly aware of some unusual aches—not unpleasant ones—in her body, which still glowed from the rough intimacy of their love-making.

'If Liam wakes I like to be there.'

'Of course you do,' she responded contritely, immediately remorseful for her clinging-vine imitation. 'I understand Liam comes first.' It would be nice to know I was a contender for one of the medal positions though, she mused wistfully.

She rolled onto her back and, bringing her knees to her chest, pulled herself briskly into a sitting position. Josh didn't strike her as the sort of man who enjoyed clingy women—probably ran a mile when he saw one coming. She squared her shoulders and gave her version—and pretty good it was, if she said so herself—of the definitive non-clingy smile.

'What?' he asked, his brow forming a censorious frown. 'No humble apology for keeping me up past my bedtime…no pun intended?'

Startled, she encountered the mocking indulgent glow in his eyes—he knew what she was doing and he was laughing at her. Nobody had ever accused her of being transparent before—could he read her mind? He certainly managed to anticipate her needs with spectacular success. With a wryly self-conscious grin, she retracted the toe she'd already placed on the floor.

'Crude pun, *you*! *Never!*' she gasped, her voice oozing sweet malice.

She yelped as Josh's hand shot out to grasp her foot mid-air; his reflexes really were remarkably well tuned. For a moment he looked thoughtfully at the graceful arch of her foot before drawing it decisively to his mouth. All the time his eyes were on her face, watching the delicate fluctuations of colour, seeing the startled little gasp form when his lips touched her flesh.

'You're gorgeous, quite literally from head to toe.' His eyes touched her tousled blonde mop of silky hair.

The rasp of his vibrant voice was like a caress; a responsive quiver shuddered through her. Almost frightened by the intensity of her desire for him, Flora obeyed his gentle but firm encouragement and wriggled her bottom along the mattress until she was able to sit on his lap and wrap both her long legs around his waist.

'I thought I was coming on too str...'

He held up a finger to his lips to still her explanation. 'I know what you thought, but don't bother killing yourself being casual and undemanding, angel. I don't feel particularly casual myself...'

'*Really!*'

'Also,' he announced with unapologetic arrogance, 'I'm a fairly demanding bloke. Actually, I've rarely felt less casual,' he announced starkly.

'That's...'

Josh grew rapidly impatient with her gobsmacked silence. 'The best joke you've heard in ages? Food for thought…? Scary…*what*…?' She was staggered to see that Josh's habitual cool had deserted him totally.

'You know, you're nearly as conceited as I thought,' she told him, rubbing a loving finger softly along the deep frown-line between his eyes. 'I'm crazy about you, you silly man.' He must have been walking around with his eyes closed if he hadn't noticed that! 'I didn't think I was being *that* subtle.'

As fast as things were going, she thought, on sober reflection, that it might be too soon, despite Josh's surprisingly upfront admission that his feelings ran a lot deeper than shallow, to throw explosive words like *love* into the conversational melting pot just yet.

The tantalisingly dominant, but too brief touch of his firm, warm lips against hers left her craving more despite their recent love-making. 'You know something.' He cupped her face between his big clever hands. 'You're *absolutely* nothing like I thought you would be. In fact, I couldn't have been further off the mark.' He shook his head as if he couldn't comprehend his own short-sightedness.

Flora raised herself up on her knees and, grabbing hold of the old-fashioned brass bed frame, deliberately pressed her breasts against his chest, which expanded dramatically as he gasped for breath. The fierce, earthy gleam in his eyes made her whimper low in her throat.

'I can see how you might have thought I have criminal tendencies,' she reflected, thinking back on their inauspicious meeting, 'but I don't go around letting down tyres every day,' she promised him, licking her finger and crossing the approximate area of her heart with a wobbly finger. 'Honestly.'

Something flickered in his eyes that made her stop. 'But you didn't mean that, did you?' Of course he'd seen her before and why not? So had half the population of the country. Her face and name had been plastered on TV screens and every tabloid front page in the country.

'You already knew about my father and the court case,' she said blankly. Wondering why it had taken her so long to realise this, she settled back down onto her heels.

'Yes, Flora, I knew.'

'I don't think much of your choice of reading material,' she joked feebly, before a hurt furrow reappeared on her brow. 'I don't understand... Why didn't you say?' She puzzled briefly before her face cleared and her hunched shoulders relaxed. 'Sorry.' She touched the side of his face gently with her hand. 'I sort of forgot some people actually have a modicum of sensitivity. Sad, isn't it?' she mused. 'I got so used to everyone acting as though me and my life were public property that when someone shows some kindness I get confused.'

'I wasn't being kind, Flora.' He spoke so harshly her hand fell away. 'I made as many snap judgements as the next man in the street about you—maybe more,' he grated. 'So have a care when you place me on a pedestal I'm woefully unsuited to.'

The warning in his voice made her shiver. 'I prefer you in my bed.' Her sally didn't draw an answering smile.

'The only difference between them and me is that I got to know the real Flora.'

'Don't beat yourself up over this, Josh,' she urged. 'We've all believed cruel lies, or skilfully edited half-truths we read in newspapers, myself included.'

Self-contempt flared in his eyes as he scrutinised her beautiful, troubled face. 'God help you, angel, but I'm probably falling in love with the real Flora.'

The colour seeped dramatically from her face. 'You are?' she croaked. He didn't look as if he was joking; then again he didn't look as though love was making him deliriously happy either!

'Nothing's one hundred per cent certain in life, but I wouldn't go laying any bets against the sort of odds we're talking here.' His expression hadn't altered; he continued to watch her with the same wary expression in his silver-shot eyes.

'I don't think it would matter what the odds were,' she reflected slowly, 'which in itself is strange because I've always been the last person anyone would have called a risk-taker...play it safe Flora, that's me. I'd still want to take a shot at making this thing work, Josh, even if we had everything and everyone conspiring against us,' she declared stubbornly.

It's taken me a long time to lose my heart to anyone, but now I'm going the whole way and then some! Part of her was appalled by her frank, no-holds-barred demonstration of faith; another part of her found the experience oddly liberating.

The conflict Josh's mobile features had been clearly displaying was supplanted by a white-hot flare of male gratification as he listened to her impassioned words.

'You sound very fierce.'

'I feel very weak,' she told him honestly. What woman wouldn't when straddled across the lap of a man with a body like Josh's? Her eyes glided warmly admiring over his athletically sculpted frame; perfect harmony was the only description that came close to summing up the muscle ratio of his impressive proportions. Deeply debilitating desire flowed through her veins.

'A weak, wanton woman...I like it.'

'That's what I want to do,' she whispered huskily.

'What do you want to do, Flora?'

Her eyelids felt heavy as the heat which pervaded her body spread. 'Whatever you like,' she explained languidly.

The sibilant hiss of his sharp inhalation cut the silence like a knife. 'My God, Flora...' His voice sounded as shaky as the hand he curved around the back of her head. She gave a slow, sultry smile as he pulled her face to his. 'Have you got the faintest idea what you're doing to me?'

'From where I'm sitting,' she announced innocently, 'it's hard to miss what I'm doing to you.'

A strangled laugh rumbled in his chest, only his eyes weren't laughing—they were filled with intense, raw need. The earthy sexuality of that look made the teasing expression fade abruptly from her own face. Nervously she ran her tongue over her suddenly dry lips.

His hands spanning her waist with casual ease, he drew her up onto her knees and then, eyes still holding hers, brought her smoothly and decisively downwards again. The corded sinews stood out in his neck as his eyes closed and his head jerked back. His mind blanked and his arousal grew even more intense as he adjusted to being sheathed within the hot, moist tightness of her receptive, eager body.

'You want me...?'

A low, needy moan emerged from her throat. She couldn't speak—hell, she'd forgotten how to breathe! She could feel, though—every atom of her being was concentrated with mindless hunger on the incredible sensation of being intimately melded with him.

Each slow, controlled thrust of his body turned her insides molten and pulled her inner muscles and nerve-endings tantalisingly closer to the release they screamed for. Her fingers dug into the resistant muscles of his shoulders as her forehead came to rest against his. His face was a dark, unfocused blur, and his breath, hot and fast, mingled and merged with her own shallow gasps just as they were merging...becoming one.

He shouted her name at the moment of climax and Flora, still with her arms linked around his neck, felt her body go suddenly flaccid with the shock of release. She loosed her grip and Josh lowered her slick, hot body gently to the bed.

Propped up on one arm, he watched the shallow rise and fall of her small breasts. He ran a finger through the delicate valley the twin soft mounds formed. Flora's eyelashes lifted from the curve of her cheek. She had never in her blissful ignorance imagined that loving someone could make a person want to weep. It was the most overwhelmingly intense feeling she'd ever experienced in her life.

'I know you've got to go.'

'Soon,' he admitted softly. 'But not yet. I want to look at you a while, and maybe hold you.'

The tender expression on his face brought the tears even closer to the surface. 'I thought men didn't go in for that sort of thing,' she teased in a wobbly voice.

'Depends on the man...and the woman he's with. On second thoughts,' he added, retrieving the tumbled sheet from the bottom of the bed and drawing it up over her still-quivering thighs, 'perhaps it would be sensible to hold back on the holding bit...considering the time restraint...' he added in response to her look of enquiry.

'I'm glad you find me irresistible but I think, under the circumstances,' she remarked drily, 'it would be quite safe. Unless, that is, you're superhuman.'

'That,' he told her, his eyes gleaming naughtily, 'is a challenge I'd love to rise to on another occasion when I'm not obliged to love you...'

'Twice,' she couldn't resist adding with dreamy-eyed complacence.

'Being the modest type, I wasn't going to labour that point.' He loftily ignored her hoot of derisive laughter. 'However, if we're talking stamina...'

'I'm sure your staying power is tremendously impressive...for a man of your age.' She ducked under the sheet with a sly chuckle.

Flora was hopelessly outmatched in the resultant wrestling match but this didn't hamper her enjoyment of the rough and tumble playfulness. Love-making and laughter had never seemed compatible bedfellows to her before, she reflected, finally pleading breathlessly for mercy.

'It's unscrupulous of you to take advantage of the fact I'm ticklish,' she protested, pushing several wayward strands of hair from her hot face and grinning reproachfully across at him.

Her glance flickered downwards to where her limbs were still snarled in a deeply satisfactory tangle with his long, long legs. Her skin looked very pale against his darker hair-sprinkled flesh; a strong, athletically built young woman, she was amazed how delicate she appeared up against him. The stark contrasts between them excited her even in her present satiated state.

'I'm a very unscrupulous man, Flora.'

He had stopped smiling and her own smile became uncertain; there had been an odd, indefinable but distinctly sobering note in his voice.

'I'd better be going.' He rolled away from her onto his back and in a single fluid motion rose from the rumpled bed.

Flora nodded, unable *not* to watch him as he padded with unselfconscious grace across the room, pausing to retrieve several garments as he did so. He really was magnificent! She couldn't figure out what had broken his mood, but something definitely had.

'Not up for milking in the morning, I hope.'

Josh fastened the last button on his shirt across his chest. 'Not until the evening tomorrow, and that'll probably be the last time. Huw's plaster is due off. Actually I promised Liam I'd take him to the beach in the morning for a picnic, a sand-in-your-sandwich sort of affair.' His long lashes lifted as he looked at her. 'Wondered if you'd like to come?'

'Sand is my favourite sandwich filling,' she replied, hoping she was managing to match the insouciant tone he'd set. Hopefully he wasn't as indifferent as he sounded.

He nodded and didn't look displeased by her reply. Flora felt content with this. It would be plain daft to start getting neurotic every time she didn't understand his mood. Josh was a very complex man, which was good as well as occasionally frustrating. Being lovers required no great effort on her part—what after all could be simpler than pleasing Josh and being pleased by Josh? The intimacy of being genuine friends seemed a much harder aim to achieve, and she wanted—*really* wanted to be his friend, not just his lover. She wanted the sort of friendship that would endure. Right now, though, she was concentrating on the important things—things such as he'd said he was falling in love with her. That was what mattered.

'I'll pick you up around eleven.'

The hard kiss he dropped on her unsuspecting lips was not at all indifferent, which proved conclusively to her how justified her optimism had been.

Flora only risked immersion ankle-deep in the sea and even that gave a nasty jolt to her nervous system—it was like ice. She worked up a healthy glow though, chasing an incredibly active three-year-old around the large beach, which was empty but for the odd person or two walking dogs or jogging.

'Enjoying yourself?' Josh caught her by the arm and swung her around. His eyes skimmed warmly over her lightly flushed features. 'Or are you lusting after Caribbean sunshine?'

The only lusting she was doing was after him. 'Caribbean sunshine has its place, but just now I wouldn't exchange five-star service and rum punches for being right here with you and Liam.' Her cheeks grew self-consciously pink as his scrutiny intensified. Her shoulders lifted. 'Call me strange...'

'I'd prefer to call you—oh, God, no!' He broke off and groaned at the crucial moment. It seemed she was never destined to hear what he would have called her—he was looking past her towards a diminutive figure heading very decisively in the direction of the water's edge. 'You can't take your eyes off him for a second!' he yelled, hitting the sand at a run.

Flora couldn't keep up with his long-legged pace and by the time she'd reached the strip of hard wet sand, rippled where the tide had recently retreated, Josh and son had emerged from the water.

'He just flung himself in head first,' Josh informed her, torn between laughter and horror as he struggled to contain his son who seemed determined to repeat his experience. 'He hasn't got an ounce of fear in his body,' he observed in a distracted, but proud parent manner.

With Flora laughter won out; she chuckled out loud as the two came nearer. Josh's capable hands were full of struggling toddler as he impatiently puffed an errant hank of dark hair from his eyes.

'I'm glad you find it funny,' he observed with a disgruntled snort.

'Well, you do look funny,' she informed him honestly. 'And there was no harm done.'

'Thanks.' He glanced down at his moleskin trousers which were wet as far as mid-thigh. 'As for no harm done, I doubt very much if these will ever be the same again.'

'And I'm sure you'll really lose sleep over that.' Josh didn't strike her as the sort of man who listed sartorial elegance very high amongst his priorities, but then he, lucky chap, looked better in the most commonplace comfy casuals than most guys did in the most up-to-date designer gear. 'I strongly suspect that you have slobby tendencies.'

'It's starting already, is it?' He raised his eyes heavenwards in appeal. 'I ask you, is it a sin for man to put comfort before fashion?'

'What?' She took off her fleece jacket and tucked it firmly around the drenched youngster who was already looking a bit blue around the edges. The fresh wind made her shiver as it penetrated the thin shirt she wore underneath.

'You want to make me over, make me presentable for all your smart, slick city friends,' he teased reproachfully.

'Huh, it would take more than a suit to do that.' Chin resting on her fingertips, she gave him a thoughtful once-over. 'Yes, *much* more than a suit.'

Actually she could think of several women of her acquaintance who would drool openly if they saw him at this precise second, with his dark wind-whipped hair all deliciously mussy and those trousers clinging like a second skin to the muscular outline of those thighs. On second thoughts, not some...all!

Josh gave a lopsided grin. 'Cow,' he observed affectionately as they puffed their way up the beach.

His puffs were due to the fact his burden didn't want to be rescued, whereas Flora suspected hers had more to do with her lack of fitness. She thought regretfully of the expensive gym she'd joined and never actually attended above twice. I'll turn over a new leaf, she promised herself.

'I think we'll just have to play the arty card. Genius is the dispensation for a lot of things, including not shaving…but then I'm sure you already know that.'

Josh placed his unhappy son on the soft sand. He lifted a hand to his square jaw. 'Actually I did shave; by mid-afternoon it's always back.'

'I'd noticed.' Her stomach muscles did a quick butterfly hiccough as she recalled the abrasive quality of his skin against her own when he'd kissed her.

'Perhaps I should grow a beard…?' he suggested innocently.

Her eyes widened in mock alarm. 'Perhaps you shouldn't, not if you want to carry on being seen with me,' she responded firmly. A girl had to draw the line somewhere.

'So shallow,' he sighed.

'I'm just not crazy about unrestrained facial hair. How would you feel if I stopped waxing my legs?'

'Severely lacerated?' he speculated.

'You're hilarious!' She was pretty sure he was disputing the point out of sheer bloody-minded cussedness; fortunately Liam distracted him before the argument got even more silly.

'Swim!' the child insisted loudly. His soft baby chin developed a distinctive stubborn tilt as he glared disapprovingly at his father.

'Not now, Liam.'

'Swim…swim!' Lying down on the sand, he began to drum his heels in time with his escalating demands.

Ignoring the synchronised display with the air of a man who'd seen it all before, Josh scooped up the rigid child and strode back towards the four-wheel drive that was parked on a gravel area just above the banks of long spiky grass that fringed the beach.

'Ordering groceries on the net is a godsend when your kid is going through the tantrum stage. Mind you, I'm assuming it's a stage. Occasionally I have this vision of a strapping fifteen-year-old lying down on the floor and screaming until he's blue in the face when I tell him to do his homework.'

'Heavens, no,' she soothed, 'teenagers have *much* more effective ways of punishing cruel parents.'

'I can hardly wait! What a little ray of comfort you are, Flora,' he breathed drily.

He placed Liam in the back seat before sliding in himself.

'Could you get the spare change of clothes from the back?'

Between the two of them they managed to strip the wet clothes off the unco-operative, already chilled child and replace them with a dry warm set.

'Pity I didn't think to pack a spare set for myself.'

'Great pity,' she agreed, letting her limpid blue gaze rest on his distracted face. 'I wouldn't mind undressing you in the back seat.'

Josh abruptly stopped what he was doing. 'I can't say the idea doesn't interest me.' The pair of sodden dungarees in his hand dripped unnoticed onto the leather upholstery as he allowed himself to match a mental image to her words.

'Lucky for you it does,' she retorted bluntly, 'or I'd be out this door.'

'Only if I let you go,' he rasped, his eyes darkening as they came to rest on her face.

This confident announcement made her pulses quicken.

Flora swallowed past the sudden constriction in her throat. She still couldn't get her head around the swiftness with which they could be transported in a heartbeat from a relatively calm, companionable atmosphere into a sexually charged maelstrom that left her panting—quite literally panting, as it happened just now! She made a conscious effort to still the agitated rise and fall of her tingling bosom.

'How do you think you'd stop me?'

'Oh, I reckon I'd think of something.'

She snorted without conviction and dragged her eyes from his smouldering scrutiny. 'Shouldn't we get Liam back? It's getting late.'

'Coward,' Josh taunted gently, but his glance followed her affectionate scrutiny in the direction of the rosy-cheeked and now sleepily placid toddler in his arms.

As Flora watched Liam's head flopped sleepily onto his father's chest. Stubbornly he jerked upright once more.

'He can hardly keep his eyes open.'

'But he'll try,' Josh predicted, strapping his son into a child restraint. 'He's as obstinate as a mule. Sometimes the only way I could get him to sleep when he was tiny was popping him into the car and driving around until he went off.' He gave a shudder.

'I can't imagine where he gets that from...' Genetics had a lot to answer for. The thought pushed home hard the nagging knowledge that she'd never have the opportunity to see what their combined genes might produce. She tried to ignore the bleak little cloud that settled around her heart. Determined not to allow anything to spoil what had been a perfect day, she vowed to concentrate on what she *did* have, not what she didn't!

'Is this brother of yours stubborn too?' Flora wondered

curiously as they both climbed into the front seat, leaving Liam to fight sleep behind them.

'Jake…? Depends on who you ask. When he and Nia fight the sparks really fly.'

'But they have a good relationship…?' she wondered with a frown. 'I mean, they're happy?'

'Are your eyes blue?' he responded drily. 'I've been thinking I've outstayed my welcome with Jake's in-laws…' The expectant silence lengthened as did Flora's tension.

It wasn't so much what he'd said but the way he'd said it that convinced her he was leading up to something. It's been nice knowing you, but…? She gave a tiny angry shake of her head. When did I get so damned insecure? she wondered. Being in love was like a white-knuckle ride and she'd never been able to see the attraction of deliberately exposing yourself to that sort of gut-grabbing fear.

'It doesn't seem that way to me,' she retorted lightly. 'They seem to treat you like a favourite son.' Continued speculation about what was coming next made her feel deeply uneasy.

She knew that inevitably they'd both have to return to their proper lives—understanding partners aside, her own sabbatical couldn't be extended indefinitely. In some ways what they had together had more in common with a holiday romance. Would they find their lifestyles were totally incompatible back in the real world? Was he already having second thoughts? She tried to let the tension seep away, but her spine remained stubbornly rigid as she waited for him to speak.

'That's on account of me being Jake's brother and since he—with a bit of help from Nia—has turned them into grandparents he can do no wrong.'

'I think it's possible they like you, for some inexplicable

reason, for being you,' she snapped, irritated by his false modesty, and worried—despite a brisk internal pep talk—about where this was all leading.

'Like you do?'

'No,' she denied, shaking her head vehemently. 'Not at all like I do!'

Josh thought about that as he pulled the car to one side to enable a wide farm truck to pass. He shot a swift searching sideways glance towards her clear-cut profile as he pulled out of a passing place on the narrow single track road he was negotiating.

'Meaning you don't like me...?'

As if he didn't know...! Cheeks flushed, she threw him an exasperated, hot-cheeked glare. 'I think we've established I like you far too much for my own good—when, that is, I don't want to strangle you!'

Josh's smug expression suggested he was well satisfied by her murderous intent. 'I've decided to put my cottage—the one Liam and I live in—on the market,' he announced abruptly.

'Oh!' This was the last thing she'd been expecting.

'When Bridie and I bought it we hadn't the faintest idea how much space kids need.' Practicality had actually played no part during the heart-searching that had gone into this symbolic gesture.

Flora hadn't missed the symbolism. 'The place must hold a lot of memories...'

He didn't bother denying her quiet observation. 'Good and bad. I've known it was time to move on for some time now but it never seemed to be the right moment.'

Flora wondered if wishful thinking was guiding her hand as she excitedly filled in the blanks left by his amazing announcement—sometimes her optimism got out of hand. 'But it is now?' she prompted carefully.

'I'll never forget Bridie, but I know now that I'm not rejecting her and what we had by getting on with my life. I think the time has come to look towards the future. Hell, I can't believe I just said anything so amazingly trite!'

'If it's any comfort, I can't believe I'm crying over something so amazingly trite.' She sniffed gruffly. Failing to discover a tissue on her person, she rubbed the back of her hand across her damp face.

'What I'm trying to say is, I'd like you to be part of that future.'

'With the proviso I don't break the rules and start getting broody.' She shot a sneaky glance in Josh's direction. He was looking pretty remote all of a sudden—*and I'm surprised*...! Why the hell did I have to go wreck the moment?

'I'm sorry, Flora, but that's the way I feel.'

It wasn't as if she wanted a baby this precise second, it just made no sense to her to rule out the possibility so totally. His intransigence made her want to scream, stamp her feet and do all manner of immature emotional things, but she didn't.

'Just checking.'

'I've been doing some checking myself on houses. Perhaps at some point in the future when you're comfortable with the idea...'

'Josh, are you asking me to move in with you?'

'No...at least, not immediately. You have to appreciate that I come as a package deal...'

Flora twisted around in her seat and smiled softly at the sleeping figure of the other half of the package. 'That hadn't escaped my notice.'

'I think that's something you should think about very carefully.'

'What is it with you?' she demanded hotly. 'You say

something nice and in the next breath you try and snatch it back. I'm falling in love with you, Flora, but if you want babies look for another man. Move in with me, Flora, but you lack the maturity to accept my child!' Her impassioned voice stilled, but only long enough for her to catch her breath. 'It's as if you're looking for some reason why this won't work,' she accused, finding there was a definite pattern to his behaviour.

'Maybe,' he suggested heavily, 'I don't think I'm good enough for you.'

'Pooh!' she mocked. 'Humble really doesn't suit you— you're arrogant down to your little cotton socks. You're well aware of your own worth on the open market.'

'It does a man's ego no end of good to be discussed like a piece of meat.'

'Don't go all politically correct and prissy on me, Josh, you know exactly what I mean. Talk about mixed signals!' she grumbled. 'Small wonder I'm confused. Let's get this straight—do you actually love me and do you want me to live with you?'

'Wow! I bet you have the opposing counsel trembling when they have to come up against you in court!'

'Don't try and sweet-talk me, Josh.'

'Fine!' he flung in a goaded voice. 'Yes, on both counts. Suddenly you don't seem to have so much to say for yourself.'

'Yes, on both counts,' she breathed shakily. 'Will that do?'

'It'll do just fine.'

CHAPTER SEVEN

'I DON'T know exactly where you'll find him, Flora, but I think he said he was heading towards the lake. If you take the footpath through the woods it takes you right up to the west side of the lake, but you'll need a coat.'

Megan Jones touched Flora's arm and felt the coolness of her firm young skin through the thin cotton shirt she wore. 'Have you walked over here like this?' she exclaimed disapprovingly. 'You'll catch your death,' she admonished. 'Come along through to the fire,' she urged the young woman who just stared back at her blankly, but did as she was bid.

'There, take a seat by the fire.' She wondered worriedly where the animated creature Josh had described to her had gone. 'I offered to keep an eye on Liam for an hour or two,' she explained as Flora sat down in the chintzy overstuffed armchair. Megan's motherly eyes crinkled with pleasure as she smiled towards the small figure seated at the low table, his expression intense as he drew a childish scrawl with his jumbo-sized crayon in a dog-eared colouring book.

The child looked up and smiled his crooked little smile of spontaneous pleasure when he saw Flora. The uncanny similarity to his father smote her to the heart.

'He's a good boy, aren't you, *cariad*?' Megan clucked warmly. She looked to Flora for confirmation of this and her smile faded. The girl didn't turn her head quickly enough to hide the sparkle of tears. 'Is something wrong, my dear?'

Flora bit her lip. 'Please don't be nice to me,' she begged shakily, 'or I'll start blubbing.'

'Do you want to talk about it?'

Flora shook her head. 'Did you know Liam's mother?' she asked suddenly. The toddler had come over to solemnly give her a page he'd carefully ripped from his colouring pad. 'Thank you, darling,' she responded gruffly, kissing the top of his dark curly head.

'No, I didn't know her. Nia didn't meet Jake until several months after she'd died...tragic...' She gave a sigh. 'But life goes on,' she pointed out briskly. 'I don't think you have any need to worry about ghosts, my dear. I've never seen Josh look so happy, not that he's ever been one to go about with a gloomy face.'

Not worry about ghosts! Considering the anonymous much-read letter crammed at that moment into her pocket, the irony of that comment brought an hysterical bubble of laughter to her aching throat.

'I think I'd better go,' she rasped huskily.

With concern Megan searched the young woman's pale face before reluctantly nodding. 'If you say so.' She sighed. 'But if you're following Josh up to the lake you'll need something warm.'

Follow...it made her sound like some meek, mild little helpmate. Does everyone who's seen us together assume I'll follow Josh wherever he goes? Flora wondered angrily as she slid her arms into the overlong sleeves of a fleece-lined cagoule. It was time to disillusion the world in general and Josh in particular!

Josh lay down his sketch-pad as he saw Flora's slim figure approaching. The welcoming smile faded from his lips as she got closer and he was able to appreciate that he'd never actually seen her angry before—not *properly* angry. He was seeing it now, though—oh, boy, was he seeing it! Warily he watched as her briskly swinging arms punched the air energetically as her long, shapely legs swept her closer.

If she'd been walking across hot coals he seriously doubted she'd have registered it. He automatically rose to his feet and brushed the dust from the dry stone wall off his trousers. Wouldn't Mum be pleased if she knew her early lectures about old-fashioned courtesy had made a lasting impact on her sons? That icy fist that had grabbed his guts suggested to him it was going to take more than nice manners to get him out of this one.

Flora came to a halt just in front of him. She was burdened by the awful things in the letter, but seeing him still did the same things to her it always had done. It couldn't all be a lie...could it?

'Well, is it true?' The trembling hand she thrust aggressively under his nose held the crumbled sheets of a letter she'd received that morning. A few scraps of paper remained in her tightly clenched fingers when he took the letter from her. 'Was your wife my dad's patient?' she asked woodenly. 'Did you follow me from London?'

Josh's eyes flickered across her face briefly before his eyes returned to the typed sheets of paper in his hands.

It was the all important response she'd been watching for. That look said it all. At that moment the tiny flicker of hope inside her died. She'd known it made no sense for anyone to make up lies like the allegations in the anonymous letter. Despite this, part of her still hadn't believed it wasn't true—not until now. All the way over to confront him she'd kept telling herself over and over again that she'd have *known* if he was pretending.

'I see.' Actually she didn't see how anyone could be so calculatingly cruel. 'You just forgot to mention it.'

Eyes filled with pain, she watched Josh skim over the

contents; his dark, lean features were drawn tight across his impossibly perfect bones. Angry, yes, he was angry, but not because he was reading meddlesome malice, he was angry because it was true and she'd found out before he wanted her to—when, she wondered bleakly, had he planned the finale?

'I didn't want to hurt you, Flora.' He lifted his dark head, his expression was sombre and his eyes shone with passionate sincerity.

The sincerity really got to her, she'd had enough of his so-called sincerity to last a lifetime—probably longer!

'I thought that was exactly what you wanted to do!' she sneered scornfully. 'Oh, I appreciate my feelings were almost incidental to your plan, it was Dad you wanted to get at through me. How inconsiderate of him to die and rob you of your ultimate revenge!' She bit back a sob and flinched back, her expression registering loathing, as he reached out for her. Had he opened the champagne to celebrate whilst she'd been weeping at her father's funeral? 'I suppose you're selling your story to the tabloids in order to spare me pain.'

Gritting his teeth, Josh lowered his rejected hand awkwardly. 'I'm not selling anything!' Actually he'd sell his soul to banish the hurt in her eyes. 'You can't actually believe I'd do that.'

'Don't you think it's a bit late to play the integrity card?' she asked him bitterly.

'Do you really think I'm the sort of man who'd deliberately court that sort of notoriety?'

'So maybe that part isn't true!' she conceded carelessly. 'If only a *fraction* of the stuff in that letter is half true it's enough to condemn you.'

'Why stop with condemnation?' The revulsion in her eyes cut him like a knife. 'Why not have a bash at sentencing too…?' Her eyes suggested life wouldn't be long enough to satisfy her sense of outrage.

'Not very long ago there were a lot of things I didn't believe you'd do, but now I know different.' She saw Josh's facial muscles tighten as he heard the crisp, cold conviction in her voice. She felt spitefully pleased. The very least he could feel under the circumstances was uncomfortable—it was the sort of pleasure that made her feel sick to the stomach.

'Actually I'd have staked my life on it.' That of course was what hurt most: she'd never trusted anyone as much as she'd grown to trust this man and all the time all he'd wanted was revenge; he'd wanted to hurt her. Objectively she watched as the colour fled his face leaving his vital flesh tinged with an unhealthy grey tone. 'Now…' her hunched shoulders lifted and she gave a bitter smile '…I think maybe there isn't much you *wouldn't* do.'

'Ask yourself why anyone would write that stuff,' he pleaded urgently.

There may not be a signature but he had no doubt as to who was responsible. To think he'd imagined he had that rat of a journalist tied up every which way—this was what you got for being a complacent idiot. This was what you got for imagining she would never find out—he'd been afraid of losing her if he told her the truth and look what was happening now. His jaw tightened with determination—he *couldn't* lose her!

'I'm not an idiot.'

She gave a bitter laugh and Josh winced. If keeping quiet had been intended to spare her pain he'd seriously miscalculated.

'Under the circumstances I think you'd better cancel that claim,' she continued stiffly. 'However, even I can see the motives behind this letter were probably one hundred per cent malicious.'

'There's no *probably* about it,' he gritted.

'But that's irrelevant. It doesn't alter the facts, fact number one being you followed me with the deliberate intention of making me fall in love with you. A simple little plan, but then they're often the best, I'm told.' Her scornful blue glare raked him, daring him to deny it. Even he didn't have the bare-faced gall to do that. Though she was sure that, being the rat person he was, he'd try and wriggle out of it somehow.

'Originally I intended to get to your father through you, yes, it's true.'

'How noble of you to come clean,' she trilled caustically. 'You know the person who came up with that old chestnut, better late than never? He was an idiot.' She couldn't imagine feeling better ever again!

A rush of dark colour seeped under his pallor as he forced himself to endure the scorn in her beautiful eyes. 'That was before...before I fell in love with you, Flora.' It sounded lame even to his own ears.

She squeezed her eyes tight shut and shook her head vigorously from side to side. 'Don't you *dare* say that,' she hissed. It made her feel physically sick when she thought of him cold-bloodedly conniving—ironically it hadn't taken much conniving! He probably hadn't been able to believe his luck; she'd been a pushover! 'I seriously doubt you know what the word means,' she informed him with icy distaste.

'Yes, I do, Flora.' If she hadn't known he was lying through his straight white teeth she might have been swayed by the sheer force of conviction in his impassioned voice. 'Because I've been immensely privileged to feel this way twice in my life.' One corner of his firm mouth quivered. 'Something I didn't think could happen. I tried to hate you, despise you, told myself that you were a cold, icy woman who didn't have a heart to break. Told myself that if the system wouldn't punish your father...'

'My father was punishing himself enough to please even you!'

The colour flooded back into his face as she flung the bitter recrimination at him. 'I tried to tell myself I was justified in using you. I even believed it for a while. But the more I saw of you, the more I knew how impossible it was to hate you.'

Even cocooned in her own private hell the depth of his sincerity shook Flora. 'If you want lessons in hate,' she told him grimly, 'look no further...'

'When something bad happens in your life—something you have no control over it's...' He swallowed and drew a sharp, ragged breath. 'You feel impotent and you want to blame someone. The court case with your father meant I finally had someone to blame...'

'My father may have made a mess of his own life, but he never harmed any of his patients. Every single investigation vindicated him on that count!'

'I know that, Flora, I just couldn't let myself believe it. I *needed* to blame someone. I wanted justice for Bridie. It was crazy...irrational, but, ask anyone, I've never been noted for my logic...'

'I can understand you needed a scapegoat, even appreciate the logic behind your sick revenge. But what I don't understand is why you carried on with it after Dad died?' A dry sob caught in her throat. 'Why did you carry on pretending? Why didn't you just go away and leave me be?' Her voice deepened and shook with outraged anguish. Why did you make me love you? she wanted to scream.

Josh shook his head and ground his teeth in frustration.

It was hellish hard wanting with every ounce of his being to hold her and knowing full well she'd reject any move he made to comfort her.

'I couldn't stop loving you if I tried, Flora, and I did try, I tried bloody hard!' he admitted loudly.

'And you're proud of it,' she suggested in a choked, disgusted voice.

'Proud! I'm ashamed. If you want to know, the thought of sitting down to share a cosy family meal with your father brought me out in a cold sweat…being rational is one thing, that is quite another. I had no idea how I'd react, but he was your father and I was prepared to give it a shot.'

'I don't believe you. If your feelings for me had been even halfway genuine you'd have told me the truth.'

'Do you think I didn't try…?' he asked her hoarsely. He raked his hair with an unsteady hand. 'I started to I don't know how many times. The longer I left it, the harder it got, and then your father died and it somehow didn't seem so urgent any more. Any obstacles between us were gone.'

'He may have been an obstacle to you, Josh…' her voice shook and the tears that had welled in her eyes began to seep out '…but he was my dad.'

'I didn't see how the truth was going to do anyone any good, and I was right, wasn't I?' He bared his teeth in a savage snarl. 'If the truth be known, I couldn't bear the idea of you looking at me like…' he lifted his head, his eyes were burning '…looking at me like this,' he finished bleakly. 'As if you hate me.'

'I do hate you!' she flashed back.

'No, you don't!' he responded with equal vehemence. 'You love me, you need me as much as I need you, and if you turn your back on what we have a day will never

go by that you don't regret it. There'll be a gap in your
life where I should be! You won't be able to stand it, I
know, I tried to turn my back on you and how I felt...do
you remember?'

Flora unwillingly recalled the time when he'd seemed
to inexplicably reject her; she'd thought that was painful...only she hadn't known at the time how bad pain
could get!

She was deeply shaken by the stark images his impassioned words conjured up, but she forced herself to respond with scornful indifference. 'Very clever of you to
keep me dangling. Your problem is, Josh, that you're in
danger of confusing real life with art. The critics may have
put you on a godlike plain, but in real life you're just a
man. There are thousands...millions just like you out
there.' She could feel the wild tattoo of her heartbeat as it
thudded against her ribcage.

'I'm the only one for you, though,' he persisted with
stubborn arrogance.

What if he was right? Her mocking laughter had more
to do with protective instincts than a response to any humour she'd discovered in the grim situation.

'Even when I didn't know what a manipulative, cold-
blooded snake you were the situation was far from perfect.
A man with a ready-made family is rarely a girl's first
choice,' she told him casually. 'You're not the only one
who had qualms to overcome.' She thought about little
Liam and his lovely smile and she almost broke down and
retracted the hurtful words. Pride held her dumb.

He looked white-faced and almost haggard as their eyes
clashed and locked. It was only stubbornness that stopped
her breaking that contact. She'd selected those words to
cause him maximum pain; wasn't it good she'd done just

that? A warm tide of triumph didn't wash over her; instead the sense of joyless desolation intensified.

A nerve in his lean cheek jumped as he slowly shook his head, rejecting what she'd said.

'Besides, I want a man who can give me children of my own, and you can't or won't do that, will you, Josh?' she reminded him spitefully.

He visibly flinched as her accusation hit home. 'No, I wouldn't do that,' he confirmed quietly. His face was as hard and still as rock.

'Flora!' he called as she turned to go.

She didn't want to turn back but something in his voice overrode her will and made her limbs respond independently of her brain. On autopilot she turned around.

'I don't believe you.'

She lifted her shoulders. 'Which part, Josh? No, on second thoughts don't tell me, I'm really not that interested in anything you have to say.'

'Whew!' Sam Taverner was only half joking when he wiped invisible sweat off his brow as he walked into Flora's office. 'Mission accomplished,' he said, plonking himself down on the edge of her desk. 'How come,' he wondered out loud, 'your desk is always so neat and mine looks like a bomb site—after the bomb's gone off?'

Flora gave a smile; it was a weak distracted affair. 'It's not complicated, you're a slob. A brilliant slob,' she conceded. Fingers tightly laced, she rubbed them against the sober material of her skirt. 'What did you say?'

'I said that you were in Hong Kong and you wouldn't be back for weeks. I thought it best to be vague…'

'Hong Kong! Why Hong Kong?' she wondered.

He shrugged. 'First thing that came into my mind,' he confessed. 'My brother-in-law is always shooting off to

Hong Kong, lucky dog, it's got a nice ring to it. Besides, if lover boy decides to hotfoot it after you it'll keep him out of your hair a lot longer than if I'd said, say… Cheltenham.'

As usual Sam's actions did have a weird sort of logic. 'Yes, well.' Flora couldn't hide her impatience with this rambling explanation. 'The point is, did he believe you?' she asked tensely.

'Well, not at first, but my days in amateur dramatics came into their own. I gave the performance of my life, if you must know,' he told her modestly.

A wave of curious anticlimax hit Flora. 'And he went away?'

'You can thank me later,' her partner responded drily.

Flora gathered her addled wits and blushed. 'Sorry, Sam, it's really good of you.'

'If you ask me, Flora, my little love, you should get an injunction out on this guy.' For once her partner dropped his amiable fool persona completely. 'I mean, he could be dangerous.'

'No, he's not.'

Her partner's gingery eyebrows shot up at the note of complete conviction in her voice. 'I don't see how you can be so sure.'

'I'm sure, that's all,' she snapped. 'Josh is harmless.' Now there was a novel notion. She'd be safer if a tiger were on her trail. 'And he's not stalking me, he's just…'

'Turning up uninvited at your flat and place of work.' Sam gave a disparaging snort. 'I always thought you were a pretty good judge of character, but this! *Harmless* is not the first adjective that springs to mind to describe your boyfriend.' It made his blood run cold just to think of what would have happened if the Hong Kong story hadn't worked. It was at times like that he wished he'd persevered with the judo lessons.

'He isn't my boyfriend.'

'Why should you feel obliged to move out of your own flat? Not that we're not delighted to have you stay with us,' he reassured her robustly.

'Because I'm not into confrontation, that's why.' Also because, although she still hadn't forgiven him and never would, now her brain wasn't fogged by the fury of betrayal she had recognised several pivotal moments when he might just have been about to tell her the truth as he claimed.

The point was he hadn't and *almost* didn't make what he had done any the less unforgivable, but how long would she remember that if he started telling her he loved her— he needed her? Or, more likely, how much she loved and needed him, she mused, recalling the arrogance of his parting shots.

'You hate confrontation…since when?' Her partner didn't bother hiding his scepticism.

'Since I last confronted Josh.'

Having met the guy, Sam found he could identify with her little shudder. 'Then you haven't actually seen him since you had your…bust-up…?'

Flora smiled. She had no intention of elaborating on what had happened, and she knew that Sam, who would be acting under strict instructions from his wife Lyn to extract all the juicy details, was agog to hear more. She'd have some news for them soon that would be shocking enough to satisfy even the scandal-hungry Lyn. She still felt pretty shocked herself. What else do I feel…?

'No and I don't want to.'

This determination not to reply to a single telephone message he'd left, or answer the doorbell when he leaned on it and stayed there, had nothing whatever to do with the fact she missed him like hell, she told herself. Who am I kidding? Push come to shove, she didn't trust herself to remember how badly he'd betrayed her if she saw him again.

For her own peace of mind Flora forced herself to identify individually each evil thing he'd done one more time. She made the worrying discovery that his sins, which had seemed very obvious, had started to get indistinct and jumbled in her head. Even if she believed he loved her that didn't cancel out what he'd intended to do, she told herself severely. She couldn't afford to start going soft…!

'Well, promise me you'll think about the injunction. I mean, if he was after me I wouldn't sleep a wink.'

My skills with the old make-up palette must be a lot better than I thought if Sam imagines I'm sleeping at all.

'Rest easy, Sam, I don't think you're his type.'

'You obviously are.'

Giving a very un-Flora blush, his partner averted her eyes and started fiddling with a sheaf of papers.

'What shall I tell Lyn? Are you going to come to the theatre tonight?'

Flora sighed; helpful friends were a pain sometimes. A person couldn't even be miserable in peace. 'You know I don't like blind dates, Sam.'

'This is a blind *double* date.'

'And that makes a difference?'

'All the difference in the world. If you can't stand this guy and things get sticky, Lyn and I will be there to make the whole thing less painfully embarrassing.'

'With sales patter like that how can a girl refuse?'

'Excellent!'

'That wasn't a yes,' she protested weakly, but Sam wasn't listening to her. She watched with amused resentment as her partner, displaying a bad case of selective deafness, made a hurried exit whistling loudly and tunelessly to himself.

'Well, what do you think of him?' Lyn whispered during the interval. Her voice was muffled as she reapplied her lipstick.

'I preferred his last play.'

'I didn't mean the play, as you well know! I've got some blusher if you want some,' she added, regarding Flora's pale cheeks with a critical frown. 'Your lippie has worn off,' she added helpfully.

'No, thanks.' Flora waved aside the offer. 'And I'm not wearing any lipstick.'

Lyn looked scandalised by this casual confession, but maintained a tactful silence on the subject. 'What do you think of Tim?'

'He's very nice.' There was nothing to object to in the man; likewise there was nothing to get worked up about, nothing to set him apart from the common throng, not like... She pulled her thoughts up short of the precipice.

Lyn gave a smug little smile. 'I knew you'd like him,' she crowed triumphantly. 'I mean, he's *so* perfect I did worry that there might be something a bit...I mean, unmarried men his age with no actual deformities are pretty rare.'

'You mean they're usually gay.'

Lyn sighed and nodded. 'Such a waste,' she bemoaned. 'But Tim's not, I made enquiries.'

Flora couldn't help laughing. 'You really are impossible.'

'I'm not the impossible one. Look at you...*beautiful*!' she announced indignantly. 'You should be up to your armpits in men. I know you scare them off deliberately.

For God's sake be *nice* to Tim, and don't act too clever,' she added as an urgent afterthought.

'You know something, Lyn, you're probably on the hit list of every card-carrying feminist in town.'

Flora, under Lyn's approving eye, did smile; she didn't always know what she was smiling at as her attention showed a marked tendency to drift around the crowded foyer.

Her glass of wine was halfway to her lips when she saw him. The glimpse was only brief, before the back of a large man's head almost immediately blocked her view, but it was enough to send her nervous system into instant shock.

'Excuse me.'

She was oblivious to the startled looks of her companions who automatically craned their necks to see what she was looking at as she firmly shoved the large man out of her way. Yes, it was him, there was no mistaking the angle of that jaw. God, but he looked gorgeous in a formal dark tie.

'Look at that hair!' Lyn breathed with an envious sigh as the voluptuous redhead draped herself all over Josh.

'Look at that body!' Nice Tim breathed with a covetous sigh.

Flora *was* looking; she was looking at the way Josh pressed the redhead's hand to his lips when she ran her fingers caressingly over his cheek. She could see the way they were visually eating each other up—it was almost indecent in a public place.

She didn't actually hear Sam's anguished plea of 'Don't do this, Flora,' as she wove her way sinuously through the seething mass of packed bodies.

They didn't even notice her! She stood there with only the width of the table separating her from the couple who seemed far too engrossed in each other to notice if the ceiling fell in. Josh's dark head moved towards the red-head's ear. He said something that brought a becoming flush to her lips and a low, husky chuckle to her white throat.

It was the sexy laugh that really tipped the balance and sent Flora right over the edge. Without being sure of what she expected to happen, she cleared her throat very noisily. They both looked at her, but Flora had eyes only for Josh.

She couldn't believe it when his eyes swept over her with an expression of polite—even vaguely irritated—indifference. He didn't even have the decency to look embarrassed!

This had been the same man who had been pursuing her with passionate avowals of enduring love! Now he was acting as though he didn't know her. A small choking sound of outrage emerged from her dry throat. The irony was she had been halfway to believing him!

'It might not matter to you,' she said in a shaking voice to the redhead, 'but this man you're with is a shallow, faithless, lying rat.'

Josh began to get to his feet, an expression of cautious alarm on his drop-dead gorgeous features. 'I think there's been...'

'A mistake?' she drawled, her eyes snapping. 'Tell me about it.' So saying, she flung the contents of her glass straight in his face.

She had a brief glimpse of his white-faced shock as she placed the empty glass in his hand before she turned on her heel and, head held high, stalked out of the now silent foyer.

'Tissue...?'

Jake Prentice took the proffered tissue from his wife and sat slowly down. 'I've never seen her before in my life...I swear!' he told her earnestly.

'Well, you would say that, wouldn't you, my darling?'

'Listen, Nia…you're having me on, aren't you?' he said, heaving a sigh of relief. 'You do believe that she was a mad woman.'

His wife gave a serene smile. 'Lucky for you, stud, I do believe you, considering she's a *pregnant* mad woman.'

'Pregnant!' The way Jake recalled it the blonde had had a very trim midriff, but he didn't question his wife's assessment. He'd learnt that Nia seemed to know this sort of thing. She had either received an extra large dose of female intuition or she had a bit of witch in her—he suspected the latter.

His eyes opened wide. 'Josh…?'

'Sometimes, Jake, you're very slow,' she mused with a patronising little sniff.

'Sometimes, Nia, you like it when I'm very slow.' Oblivious to the fact they were the cynosure of all eyes and numerous low-voiced conversations since the blonde had departed, Jake kissed his wife very thoroughly.

CHAPTER EIGHT

Josh perched on the edge of one of the many packing cases stacked in the room and watched with a resigned expression as his twin produced an outsized bar of chocolate from his pocket for Liam. Predictably his son went into transports of chocoholic delight.

'Ever heard of a balanced diet?' he enquired as Liam threw a fit—the noisy variety—because his mean dad had exerted a bit of parental control and confiscated the biggest portion of the foil-wrapped bar.

'That stuff's a parent's province, I'm his uncle... Have you noticed how little Liam here is one of the few people who can always tell us apart?'

'That's because he can spot a soft touch a mile off, and I'll remind you about that uncle thing when the twins have got teeth to rot,' Josh warned darkly. 'How are the twins?' he added, enquiring after his six-month-old nieces.

'Blooming, and brilliant. Why, little Angharad...'

Josh knew from experience that the soppy smile on his brother's face usually preceded a long rambling discussion concerning the perfection of his small daughters. In common with a lot of new fathers, Jake was under the impression that everybody else was as fascinated as him with every minute detail concerning his offspring. Josh was a doting uncle but there were limits to his devotion...

'It's good of Nia to offer to have Liam today,' he cut in quickly.

'Least we could do, considering moving house is supposed to be right up there with the most stressful things in life…which would account for the fact you look like hell,' his brother mused slyly. 'It *would* account for that, wouldn't it, Josh?'

It might, after all, have been less tiresome to let Jake ramble on about the babies. Josh resisted the urge to tell his brother to mind his own damned business—he knew from experience it wouldn't do any good—and contented himself with grunting unhelpfully.

'Where's Nia?'

'In the car, she didn't want to ruin a male bonding moment. And, before I forget, I've got something for you.'

The casual mention of male bonding brought a suspicious frown to Josh's brow as he looked down at the piece of paper his twin had pressed into his hand. 'What's this?'

'As you see, a bill.'

Josh turned the innocuous scrap of paper over. 'Your dry-cleaning bill?' Bizarre even by his twin's standards.

Jake nodded in confirmation. 'Wine, the shirt was a write-off…' he elaborated sadly.

'I'm sure you're going to get to the punchline eventually. The thing is…' Josh glanced pointedly at his watch '…I don't have all day.'

'Save the sarcasm. I would have sent it to the lady, but I don't know her address—I expect you do…'

'Will you stop being so enigmatic?'

'The lady in question was tall, blonde, attractive—*very* attractive actually,' Jake conceded thoughtfully. 'Ring any bells?' He saw his brother stiffen. 'But if Nia asks, I didn't notice the attractive part.'

'Where…? When…?' Taking a deep breath, Josh regained control—at least partially. 'What did she do?' he asked tensely. Wine over a dinner jacket implied clumsiness or a defensive act of sorts—Flora didn't have a clumsy bone in her body. 'What did you do to her?'

Jake held up his hands. 'Hold up, boy, you're looking at the victim of the piece. Does *she* have a name? We didn't really reach the polite exchange stage.'

'Flora.'

Jake did his wide nod thing, the one that always irritated Josh. 'Nia thought it must be…'

'How did Nia…?' Josh exploded. 'Ah, Megan,' he grunted in a disgruntled tone. Was the concept of a private life totally alien to his family?

'Your Flora verbally abused me and then chucked her wine over me…it was red, actually,' Jake elaborated with a fastidious shudder. 'All this, I might add, was done in front of my wife, not to mention a captive audience of what felt like thousands.'

For a split second the grimness of Josh's expression was lightened by a light of unholy glee as he imagined how much his twin would have hated this public humiliation, although admittedly Jake had lightened up considerably since his marriage. His amusement speedily faded when it hit home that the attack and the humiliation had been meant for him!

My Flora, she is *my* Flora—the inescapable certainty of this ran bone-deep in him. It was just convincing her of the fact that presented the problem! His jaw tightened with determination. Wasn't it just ironic that he'd been scouring the city for her, virtually camping on her doorstep, and it was Jake who got to see her?

He glared resentfully at his twin. 'She thought you were me?'

'The thought doesn't make me happy either, but it seems a fair assumption. It's certainly not an effect I usually have on women, but then my social life has never been half as interesting as yours, brother dear.'

'You mean you've always been a dull, virtuous stick-in-the-mud.'

Jake displayed no sign of offence as he shrugged off the insult. 'It may have escaped your notice, Josh, but you've been equally dull and virtuous for several years now. I hate to be the one to break it to you, but most people have forgotten you even had a misspent youth! Don't you think it's time you stopped trading on your youthful hell-raising image? If you ask me...' he continued thoughtfully.

'Which I wasn't...'

'She was jealous.'

Josh suddenly looked a lot more interested in what his twin was saying. 'You think so...' he began, trying not to sound too eager and failing miserably.

'Nia was being quite affectionate at the time,' Jake informed him cheerfully.

'*Must* you be so smug?' Josh complained out of habit rather than conviction. 'We all know you're the perfect husband and father, you tell us often enough.' If Jake was right—which he had an irritating habit of being—then that opened up all sorts of interesting possibilities...

'I'll have you know that Nia holds you up as the ultimate example of the perfect dad ad nauseam...' his twin responded indignantly.

'I'd say she was a woman of taste, but she married you...'

'If you want...'

'The benefit of your worldly wisdom,' Josh cut in sarcastically. 'I don't. I don't know what makes you think you have the right to interfere with my personal life?' he growled, displaying a complete lack of gratitude for the brotherly concern.

'What a woefully short, amazingly selective memory you have,' Jake drawled. 'I seem to recall someone lying through his teeth to get me together with Nia, not to mention locking me in a room with her! I didn't notice you displaying any reluctance then or ever to interfere in *my* personal life!'

Josh conceded the point with a reluctant grin. 'Like you wanted to escape! Anyhow, you've always been a complete loser with women; without my help you'd still be a crusty old bachelor.'

'Old!' Jake protested. 'What does that make you?'

'Some people are born old.'

'Well, at least no woman has ever thrown wine in my face...at least not knowing it was me.'

Josh's expression sobered as he announced abruptly, 'She's Graham's daughter, you know.'

He did his best not to recoil from the glimmer of sympathy in Jake's eyes as his twin slowly nodded. It didn't really come as a shock to see Jake displaying no signs of incredulity; he'd suspected from the outset that his brother knew more about the situation than he was letting on.

'I did catch some of her previous public appearances, but the drastic change of style threw me a bit—icy composure to spitting fury...?' Jake let out a silent whistle.

'Was she alone?' Josh found he couldn't dismiss the disturbing thought that Flora might have been with another man from his mind.

'Well, her regal exit was a strictly solo affair, not that that means much. It's not actually very likely she went to the theatre alone.'

'Thanks for nothing.'

'Well, I didn't actually see anyone, but then if I'd been with her I'd have been hiding too,' Jake admitted frankly.

'I'm going to marry her.'

'Don't tell me, tell her.'

'What do you think I've been trying to do?' Josh yelled.

'It doesn't make any difference who her father was,' he added aggressively.

'Obviously not.' It would have taken a more reckless man than himself to contradict Josh in his present volatile mood. 'I take it you are seeing things a bit clearer in the Graham area these days?'

'I am, but Flora doesn't believe it, with some justification,' Josh admitted. 'A hell of a lot of justification, actually.'

'So you were still on a revenge trip when you took off without a word to anyone and ended up with my in-laws?' His twin gave a grudging nod of assent. 'And your motives for getting involved with the lady weren't originally entirely pure,' Jake surmised.

'What exactly did she say to you?' Josh barked, looking ready and willing to squeeze the information out of his sibling if he didn't voluntarily cough it up.

'Nothing that wasn't cryptic and damned right insulting—you two obviously have a lot in common—I'm just making an educated guess. Come along and see Aunty Nia, Liam,' he coaxed, kneeling down and holding out his arms for the toddler to climb into. Liam ignored his uncle with a sweet but stubborn smile and continued to smear chocolate over the remaining clean parts of his face.

'Talk about *déjà vu*,' Jake mumbled. That grin was identical in every way to the one his twin had frequently used to get his own way through their formative years together. If there was any justice in the world Josh would be in for a taste of his own medicine over the coming years.

'Actually I've made a real dog's dinner of this, Jake.'

His expression sober, his twin got to his feet. 'I had gathered that much, I'm just amazed that I'm hearing you admit it, Josh. What are you going to do?'

'Damned if I know, she's made it crystal clear she can't stand the sight of me.'

Jake regarded with a frown the uncharacteristic dejected slump of his brother's shoulders. He was beginning to feel quite concerned about his twin's state of mind. He needed shaking up a bit.

'I always knew you were a closet romantic, Josh, but I never knew you were a wimp!'

Josh, his expression one of seething frustration, grabbed his twin by the shoulders and glowered dangerously into eyes remarkably similar to his own. The hot fire died away as quickly as it had erupted. A grim expression on his face, he released the creased fabric of his brother's top.

'God, that's me, sensitive new age man,' Josh bit back angrily.

'You've made your point,' Jake conceded wryly with a weak grin as his brother flexed his not inconsiderable shoulder muscles. 'You're no wimp, just an idiot. Actually, there's something you might like to take into consideration when you're deciding what you're going to do next.'

'Which is?' Josh asked, kissing his son's brow and handing him over to his uncle with a firm, 'Be good for Aunty Nia, champ.'

'*Aunty* Nia says your Flora's pregnant.'

Jake watched sympathetically as his big, tough brother clutched towards the wall for support. 'She can't be,' he croaked after a short, painful pause.

'You'd be in more of a position to know about that than me, but personally I wouldn't bet against Nia's intuition.'

'*Well?*' Nia prompted impatiently when her husband returned carrying their nephew.

'Well what?'

'Were you kind and gentle?'

'Kind and gentle would have *really* put his back up.'

'And I suppose nasty and sarcastic didn't!'

'What was I supposed to do...cuddle him?'

Nia rolled her eyes. 'Now wouldn't *that* be shocking?' she observed waspishly. Men! To hear the pair of them talk you'd never know they'd each walk through fire for the other.

Well, there was no point her hiding out in Sam and Lyn's spare room any longer—Josh had obviously given up trying to contact her. It was just as well she already knew Josh's so-called love was a hollow sham otherwise the fact that his devotion had strict geographical limits—and Hong Kong was outside them—might have come as a blow.

It wasn't as if she'd expected him to hop on the first available flight, but he might have waited for a semi-decent interval before hopping into bed with the first available female! She gave a tiny shudder of revulsion as an image of the sexy redhead materialised in her head.

Flora continued to tell herself how relieved she was that Josh had no staying power, at least in the fidelity department. Elsewhere...well, the sooner she stopped thinking about Josh Prentice's staying power *elsewhere*, the sooner she could get her life back on track!

A soft holdall looped around her neck, two more at her feet, she struggled with a recalcitrant lock.

'Damn and blast it to hell!' she cursed wearily just before the key finally clicked. With a sigh she threw her bags carelessly over the threshold and followed them.

The sound of the door being clicked shut made her swing around in alarm. Josh was standing there looking tall, dark and dangerous.

He'd hurt and betrayed her in every way possible, he'd forgotten about her when the going had got tough and yet every instinct in her told her to walk—no, to *run*—straight into his arms.

'Get out!' she yelled hoarsely, picking up the nearest thing, which happened to be a soft cushion—it bounced harmlessly off his dark head.

'In my own good time,' he soothed, rubbing the side of his head. 'That hurt.'

'I wish!' she hissed venomously. 'And you won't get out in your good time, you'll get out in mine—in other words now, if not sooner! Does the green-eyed vamp know you're here?' she asked shrilly, then, just to establish she didn't care one way or the other, she added hastily, 'I *almost* feel sorry for her.'

'The only green eyes I see,' Josh murmured with provocative pleasure, 'are right here!' He looked pointedly at her flushed face and flashing cornflower-blue eyes.

'Cut out the wisecracks—and, actually,' she added huffily with a dignified sniff, 'you couldn't be more wrong!' Even she didn't believe it, and one glance at his face told her he didn't either!

'If you don't care, would you mind explaining to me about the wine-in-the-face stunt?'

'I don't think you're in any position to gripe about my behaviour, but if you must know it was just a spontaneous expression of my deep contempt for you.'

Considering the fact she hadn't had the faintest idea what she was going to say when she opened her mouth, Flora felt moderately pleased with this glib face-saving explanation.

'I'm so sorry if I ruined your evening,' she added with spiteful insincerity.

'Actually I didn't come here to discuss the extortionate cleaning bill I've been presented with.'

'Really! I didn't think we had any other unfinished business.' If he had the bare-faced cheek to present her with a bill she'd make him eat it!

'I think you know we have.' His grey eyes moved slowly over her face with almost clinical precision as though he was searching for something specific. *'Is it true?'* he asked abruptly.

Flora froze. Her mind raced frantically—he couldn't know, she told herself soothingly. How could he when she hardly knew herself? The secret was uppermost in her mind, which accounted for the fact her powers of deduction were a bit distorted just now. If I don't volunteer anything, he can't know anything. She dabbed her tongue to her upper lip to blot up the tiny beads of moisture there.

'Is what true?' Her eyes widened to their fullest, most guileless extent.

Josh's own eyes narrowed as his glance moved from her innocent expression to the heaving outline of her chest. 'You want to play it like that...?' She watched nervously as his heavy lids drooped further over his worryingly alert gaze. 'Fine,' he approved casually.

'I don't know what you're talking about.' Please God he didn't either!

'I want to talk about us.'

She relaxed slightly, but not much—*us* couldn't be classed as a safe subject either.

She carefully wiped her face of all emotion and stared at him stonily. It would be the final humiliation if he guessed how often she had dreamt of there being an *us*...if he guessed that how, even after all he'd done to her, if she'd seen him at a pre-redhead moment she might have been tempted to try against all odds to work towards there being an *us*.

'There is no *us*, and never has been.' That should do the trick! She had put her heart and soul into sounding as though she meant it—only a completely insensitive idiot could have failed to get the message in her icy put-down.

It frustrated her beyond belief to discover his silent, vaguely amused response was loaded with teeth-clenching scepticism. How could she have forgotten that Josh *was* a completely insensitive idiot?

Ignoring her little snort of annoyance, Josh contemplated thoughtfully the set angle of her firm chin, before strolling further into the room and looking around with interest.

'Nice place you have here.' He ran the square tip of one tapering finger down the spines of a row of books in her crammed bookcase.

Her own spine reacted as though it had received the caress. Just looking at his shapely hands made her feel shivery and feverish. Anxious to dismiss these distracting sensations, she said the first thing that came into her head—unfortunately her thoughts emerged uncensored.

'Can your new girlfriend actually read, or does her bosom get in the way?' They couldn't have been real, Flora decided spitefully, thinking nasty, unsisterly thoughts about the curvaceous redhead.

His cough had started off sounding something suspiciously like a laugh. And no wonder he looked smug and self-satisfied, she thought bitterly as her tortured blue gaze slid self-consciously away from the sparkle in his amused eyes. So much for icy indifference, I might just as well have put out an advert in a national newspaper in case anyone hadn't realised I'm a jealous cat!

'Being a man...'

'I'd hardly noticed,' she said wistfully, tearing her lingering lustful gaze from his long, muscular legs.

'I would never dare make a connection between a lady's cup size and her IQ,' he explained virtuously. The saintly air was rather spoilt by a lecherous grin that suddenly split his rather hard features. 'I'm more a leg man myself,' he admitted, dropping casually into an old leather armchair.

Flora wished she'd opted for trousers—not that there was anything remotely revealing about her severely tailored skirt unless you had a thing for ankles or calves. She remembered that Josh had had a thing about just about every part of her no matter how mundane. Desire made her skin prickle as sexual heat rushed through her.

'It's my brother, Jake, who's the—'

Shamed at her weak response to him, Flora knew that she'd be a gibbering basket case if he turned his attention anywhere more intimate than her legs! Besides, she didn't want to invite any unkind comparisons with his bosomy date!

Shrilly she cut him off. 'Don't make yourself comfortable, you're not staying!' she snarled. 'If you don't stop ogling my legs,' she informed him, conveniently ignoring the fact she'd been doing the same thing herself only moments before, 'I'll...I'll...' he quirked an enquiring dark brow in her direction '...I'll call the police!' That injunction was looking more attractive by the second.

'Really! That would make interesting listening,' he reflected. 'Could you send around an armed response unit? My boyfriend is looking at my legs...'

She gnawed at her quivering lower lip as she listened to him mock her toothless threat. 'You're not my boyfriend.' Boyfriend was a much too tepid term to describe Josh; there was nothing remotely boyish about him. She hated the pushed-into-a-corner, whiny note she heard in her tremulous voice. How was he supposed to believe she meant what she said if she sounded so wishy-washy?

Josh appeared to give serious thought to her statement.

'Yes, I prefer lover too, it has a much more grown-up and...intimate ring to it.'

His deep sexy purr made all the fine downy hairs on the back of her neck prickle. She no longer worried if she was in control of the situation; she *knew* she wasn't!

'Talking about Jake...' he continued, crossing one long leg over the other. Flora noticed he was wearing odd socks. She found herself wondering if he'd had a tough night with Liam...or perhaps there was a much less innocent and possibly more likely explanation for his red-rimmed eyes and unshaven chin... She felt suddenly mad as hell—with him, with herself, with stupid, bloody-minded cruel fate that had made her fall in love with him!

Flora folded her arms firmly across her bosom. 'I wasn't, you were, but I have to tell you I'm not that interested in your family.' She produced an artistic yawn.

'Oh, Jake's quite interested in you; so is his wife, Nia.'

Flora, still coping with the most atrocious pangs of jealousy, kept her expression blank as he extracted a photo from his breast pocket and held it out to her. She automatically placed her hands behind her back and mulishly shook her head. Doing exactly the opposite of what he wanted felt extremely important to her.

'I don't want to look at your family snaps.'

'Look at it!'

'Don't you take that tone with me!' For the first time Flora saw that beneath the air of laconic, laid-back amusement Josh was actually extremely tense.

'I think you'll find it quite illuminating.'

He obviously wasn't budging until she'd done as he bid so she decided she might as well humour him. Ungraciously she snatched the glossy photo from his hand, hoping the way she carefully avoided any contact with his fingers wasn't too obvious.

She felt the blood seep from her face as she stared incredulously at the image of a radiant woman in a stunning wedding gown flanked by two amazingly handsome men wearing morning dress. Josh was one of the men, but for the life of her she couldn't tell which one!

'You're a twin!' she croaked accusingly as the colour returned to her face with a vengeance. 'You didn't tell me... *Oh, God!*' she groaned as she recalled the shocked expression on her victim's face as he'd dashed red wine from his eyes.

He'd acted as if he hadn't recognised her because he hadn't! She'd never felt so squirmingly embarrassed in her life. 'Why on earth didn't you tell me?' Fists clenched, she rounded on Josh furiously. 'If you had I wouldn't have made a total fool of myself...'

Josh took her spitting fury in his stride. 'Jake thought it was my fault too.'

'He must think I'm...a mad woman. I must be to care who you choose to canoodle in public with!' She didn't notice the white-hot flare of satisfaction in his eyes as she miserably visualised the sort of rampant speculation her little stunt must have created. With an anguished groan she buried her face in her hands. 'God, she was his wife...the one...'

'With the D cup.' He nodded solemnly as she squirmed some more. 'Yes, that's Nia.'

'She's beautiful.' Amazing how much easier it was to admit that now she knew the lady in question was married to Josh's brother, that she wasn't a rival...what am I talking about, rival?

A sudden rush of relief flooded through her. 'That means you haven't...?'

'Looked, touched or had improper thoughts even about another woman.' He shook his head solemnly from side to side. 'Innocent on all counts. Does that make you feel better?'

Flora flushed rosily. 'I could care less.' She knew her denials were futile, she just couldn't hide her feelings from him, but she felt obliged to make an effort. 'Did she—your brother's wife, think…?' Flora began in sudden trepidation. All she needed to make this day complete was to discover she was responsible for splitting up what had looked like a blissfully happy couple.

'Don't fret, all is peaceful on the marital harmony front. Nia has an exaggeratedly high opinion of my brother's integrity.'

'You mean he *would* cheat on her?' she demanded, her glare one of shocked disapproval.

'I mean I've been insulting Jake since I first mastered the knack of stringing a few words together, the habit's become ingrained. Jake would die before he'd hurt Nia, the man's besotted.'

'Well, he looked it,' Flora recalled wistfully as she recalled with horrible clarity what his besotted behaviour had done to her when she'd thought that he were Josh. 'I still can't believe there are two of you,' she murmured in a stunned voice.

'There aren't!' Josh bit back swiftly.

'Have I hit a nerve?' She didn't need any convincing; there couldn't be anybody else quite like Josh.

Josh didn't deny it. 'It's a common misconception.' His tone of voice suggested it was an irritation too. 'But we're just two people who happen to look very much alike… though I must admit I'm pretty insulted that you couldn't tell the difference. Nia could right off…but then Nia's a bit of a mystic on the side—must be the Celtic blood,' he mused. 'Talking of which, she said something about you…'

'Nothing flattering, I'm sure,' Flora reflected, blushing to recall what sort of first impression she must have made. 'But it can't be any worse than the things I've been saying about her,' she admitted guiltily.

'Jealousy will do that.'

Flora gritted her teeth. 'I can't decide if you're just plain stubborn or you really believe you're irresistible!'

'You're in denial, at least about this,' Josh qualified cryptically.

His relentless confidence made her want to scream, especially as she knew it was justified. 'Don't you ever give up?'

'Never,' he confirmed. 'Are you in denial about the other too?'

Flora's expression was distracted and confused but not suspicious. 'What other?' she enquired innocently.

'The being pregnant other.'

'Oh, God!' she gasped. She took a stumbling couple of shaky steps towards the nearest chair but the buzzing in her ears and the black dancing dots before her eyes got so bad she just folded up, cross-legged, onto the floor before Josh, who had dived in her direction as soon as the colour had dramatically fled her face, could reach her. 'How... how?'

'It's true, then.' Josh didn't know whether to join her in a collapsed state on the floor or bang his head against the wall. If he'd been using said precious head this mess wouldn't be happening! He'd done several things over the years he wasn't proud of but he'd never despised himself more than at this moment!

Flora pulled herself into a kneeling position and rested her bottom on her heels. She'd never seen anyone look so wretched and distraught as Josh did; he'd aged visibly in the last thirty seconds.

Somehow she'd never pictured the father of her first child reacting like this to the news he was about to be a father. Some romantic dreams it seemed persisted even in the face of adult cynicism, but then she always had been a hopeless romantic at heart.

'How did you know? I hardly…' Even Josh's persuasive powers were not enough to open confidential medical files.

'What can I say?' he asked hoarsely. 'My brother married a witchy woman. You may laugh…' Flora didn't feel like laughing at all '…I did myself the first time, but she definitely has a spooky ability for this sort of thing. Maybe she is just extra smart at reading body language, who knows…?' He sounded as though he didn't much care about the method he'd learnt the truth, but the truth itself was bothering him more than slightly.

Flora ran her fingers through her feathery crop and pulled herself to her feet; her expression was sober. 'I don't care what you say,' she warned him, her small chin lifted to an obstinately determined angle.

'So tell me something I *don't* know!' Josh grated harshly. 'You're not going to faint or anything, are you?' he added with gruff suspicion.

'No.' Decision glowed in her blue eyes as she bit her lip. 'I know how you feel, Josh, about having any more children—' she swallowed the constriction in her throat '…but I won't have an abortion,' she announced grimly. 'No, don't say anything!' she pleaded, placing her hands firmly over her ears. 'I can't and I won't!' she insisted loudly. 'This is my baby and you don't need to have anything to do with it.'

The mention of abortion had made what little remaining colour he had seep steadily away. His eyes burnt with anger in his otherwise immobile features as he met her defiant glare head on.

'I won't even dignify the notion I could wish any child of mine harm, let alone actively seek it with...' Flora could hardly bear it when his deep, emotion-packed voice broke.

'I thought...' she began. Seeing her outstretched hand reaching out towards him, she snatched it self-consciously back.

'I know what you thought.' The reproach in his eyes made her cheeks burn afresh with shame. 'I'm interested in how you figure that I won't need to have anything to do with my own child?'

She looked at him with undisguised scepticism. 'Are you trying to tell me that you *want* to be involved?'

That dream was quite stubbornly persistent, but there came a point, she told herself, when optimism was ever so slightly silly and as she listened to his response she knew that this was the time. The prospect of fatherhood would do what all else, against the odds, seemed unable to: it was going to make it impossible for them to be together. There weren't any workable compromises.

'*Want* isn't the right word precisely,' he began cautiously.

Flora tried hard not to flinch. 'I didn't think it was, somehow.'

'It's about responsibility. I've told you before that I turned my back on Liam briefly once, and I've never forgiven myself. I'm not about to make the same mistake twice.' The memory seemed to release a torrent of self-condemnation in him. 'If it hadn't been for Jake...'

'Not that again!' she yelled suddenly, drawing his startled gaze. 'I'm sure your brother is great, but he was only doing what brothers are meant to do in that situation. You'd do the same for him, wouldn't you?' she challenged.

'Sure,' Josh conceded. 'But you don't know it all. I drank...'

'Drank!' Rolling her eyes in exaggerated horror, she pressed her hands to her cheeks. 'Big deal! We all get hurt, we all mess up and most of us crawl back. Only I forgot Josh Prentice doesn't lose control, he doesn't mess up and he never crawls. For God's sake, man,' she told him in exasperation, 'you're a fantastic father to Liam!' She fixed him with a blisteringly sincere stare.

'Are you defending me?' he asked in a voice of wonderment.

'Only against your worse critic—you!' she announced, gruffly defiant. She tried not to think distracting thoughts about how much she'd liked it when Josh had lost control in some situations. The fact she lusted after him...loved him to bits...just made doing what she knew she had to harder—*much* harder! 'What I'm saying is no reflection on what sort of father I think you'd make.'

'It's hard to forgive yourself for...'

'Being human!' she responded with heavy sarcasm. 'The point is, I don't know how hard it will be having this baby, but I do know it would be a hell of a lot harder with you watching every move I make waiting for something bad to happen. I'm sorry if this sounds brutal, but I want to *enjoy* this pregnancy. It's something very special.'

She saw his strong throat muscles work before he finally responded. 'Are you trying to tell me that having me around would make you...?'

'Me jumpy, nervous, unhappy? Probably all three.' But not nearly as unhappy as it would make you, she thought sadly. 'I know that was your original intention.'

He flinched; his hurt eyes silently reproached her. 'I told you, Flora, that that was before I fell in love with you.'

'If you really love me, Josh, leave me alone. Let me

have the baby. I want him, you don't.' He could have denied it, but she knew he wouldn't.

The conflict on his face was only a weak shadow of his internal struggle.

'Do you really think I could abandon you and our baby?' He looked at her as though she had lost all sense of reality.

'I know you don't want him,' she wailed miserably.

'I want you, Flora. Marry me.'

CHAPTER NINE

FLORA gave a faint, wispy gasp. Her knees quivered wildly. 'You can't be serious!'

'I've never been more serious in my entire life,' he revealed grittily.

Despairingly she tore her gaze from the compelling conviction in his eyes. She shook her head slowly in denial.

'Are you mad?' she croaked, showing what she considered an amazing amount of restraint under the circumstances. 'I know you don't like feeling helpless, Josh.'

'True, but it's a theme I'm getting tiresomely familiar with of late,' he chimed in grimly.

This solution was a bit extreme even for him. 'But doing something…doing *anything*, especially *this* anything to make yourself feel as if you're in control is not a good idea.'

In control! Was she joking? 'I haven't been in control since the first moment I met you!' he declared, his resentment very obviously smouldering. He threw her a harassed, driven look. 'My life wasn't so crash-hot terrific before,' he growled. 'But at least it had some sort of comforting predictability.'

'Then you ought to be careful about who you decide to stalk in future,' she felt pushed by his perverse logic to point out.

'Hell!' He stopped, an arrested expression stealing across his dark face. 'Predictable! Like it was a good thing… *Did I really just say that?*' he appealed to her, a comically horrified expression spreading across his handsome, haggard face.

'I take it that was a rhetorical question. Or has your short-term memory gone the same way as your sanity?'

'I sound so *old*,' he announced in a shaken voice that, if she hadn't been so deeply shaken, might have made her smile. 'If I go on like this I'll be as boring as Jake before long,' he observed acidly.

'I didn't see too much wrong with Jake.' How could she when he looked so like the man she loved?

Josh shot her a sharp, not altogether pleased look. You don't say,' he responded in a disgruntled tone. 'Actually we're chalk and cheese, nothing alike, the original odd couple.'

'He sounds better by the minute,' she mumbled provocatively.

'You love me really,' he shot back carelessly, though had she seen his eyes she might have revised the careless part.

She watched, stifling her frustration and growing panic as he recommenced his monotonous pacing of the room. It was, she admitted, probably the only time she'd think monotonous in the same breath as Josh and, if she was being scrupulously honest, she liked it that way.

'I do...?' she echoed faintly. It occurred to her she ought to be objecting to this sort of cocky confidence.

He stopped his panther-like pacing and looked directly at her. Now she forced herself to analyse his expression she saw that he didn't look particularly confident, just fierce, driven and deeply distracted.

'It's blindingly obvious,' he announced. 'I love you, you love me.' Jaw clenched, chest heaving, hands balled into white-knuckled fists, he paused to let her deny it.

The significance of her silence was deafening. The pupils of his eyes visibly expanded and a bone-deep thrill shot through her as their eyes clashed and melded. *'We have to get married.'*

'Why? Do you think I'm likely to be ostracised by polite society? Grow up, Josh,' she sneered shakily.

He ignored her sub-standard attempt at sarcasm. 'You need me.'

How horribly true. Her chin went up. 'To be a martyr...thanks, but no, thanks! You've made your views on fatherhood crystal clear.'

'That was before this *fait accompli*, that changes everything.' His grim voice was laced with the crushing strain he was feeling.

Everything except the way you feel, she wanted to shout. 'This baby isn't a *fait accompli*!' she yelled. 'As hard as you obviously find it to believe, I *want* this baby.' Her intensity drew his narrowed gaze to her face. 'Until you do too you can keep away from me...us. If I do drop dead,' she flung recklessly, 'you'll have a role to play, but I have no intentio—' She didn't get any further.

He moved with astonishing fluidity for a big man. He grabbed her by the shoulders and hauled her roughly towards him until her tender breasts were pressed close to his heaving chest. His eyes blazed down at her. The rage that consumed him was a tangible thing, like static it danced in the air around them.

'Never, *never* make a crack like that again.' The soft staccato words emerged from compressed, bloodless lips. 'Do you hear me?'

Overcome with remorse, she nodded. 'I didn't mean...'

Josh released his biting grip on her. His fingers curled around the soft nape of her neck before sliding upwards across her scalp. 'I was her husband, Flora, I should have been able to save her.' The memory of that failure still haunted him, she could see it in the stark pain in his eyes, hear it in the harsh unevenness of his tone. 'I tried to blame fate, your father when the opportunity arose, but deep down I knew, I always have, that the responsibility was mine...'

'But that's...' He hushed her automatic horrified protest with a finger pressed to her lips. His words continued to carry the same implacable conviction.

'It was me who wanted to start a family straight away. Bridie just went along with what I said to please me, she always did, which was very convenient for a man who likes to get his own way.' His voice was laden with bitter self-derision. 'Her family blamed me, they never wanted her to marry me in the first place, and they were right,' he asserted grimly. 'But I won't let anything happen to you,' he vowed fiercely, threading his fingers through the bright strands of her hair.

'It already has...I fell in love with you, Josh.' She heard the hissing intake of breath, felt his chest swell and saw the flame that smouldered for a fraction of a second before igniting to an incandescent blaze in his eyes. She closed her eyes dizzily as his lips swooped downwards.

'But that doesn't matter!' she protested just as she felt the first touch of his mouth against hers. He froze. Flora felt his big strong body quiver with strain as he held back his lips still almost touching her own. She trembled feverishly; her desire for him was so strong she could taste it on her tongue.

'It doesn't matter that you love me!' he echoed in a disbelieving whisper. The warmth of his fragrant breath teased the ultra-sensitive flesh around her ear. 'That I love you...what sort of insanity is that, Flora? It's *all* that matters.'

'That's too simplistic,' she persisted tearfully, and, oh, so tempting…!

Breathing unsteadily, he brought his forehead to rest against hers. 'I know we had a bad start. Hell,' he ejaculated unsteadily, 'that's the granddaddy of all understatements! But I'll make that up to you, I promise… Can't you forget the past…?'

'I can,' she told him with sudden complete conviction. 'But you can't, Josh. Don't you see *that's* the problem?'

His thumbs moved compulsively over the smooth, firm angle of her jaw. 'Even if I accepted that, which,' he told her stubbornly, 'I don't, what's your solution—something mature like refusing to see me again? You could always have your friends tell me you'd gone to Australia this time, why mess around with half measures? Hong Kong! Did your pal really think I'd swallow that one?' he enquired scornfully. 'I warn you, Flora, it wouldn't really matter where you went to—you see, I'd follow you to the ends of the earth!'

'You would…?' Emotion clogged her throat.

'Do you doubt it?'

Looking into his eyes, she didn't. She almost heard the sound as the last threads of resistance within her snapped.

'I don't think I could not see you,' she confessed brokenly. 'I love you so much it hurts.'

Josh's head fell back and he gave a long, juddering sigh of relief. When he eventually looked down into her eyes his own glowed with heart-stopping tenderness. 'I've waited a long time to hear you say that.'

'But that doesn't mean I'm going to do anything drastic.'

Like give myself permission to be happy? She suddenly saw clearly the stupidity of her fearful stance. She had nothing to lose and everything to gain.

This is it, girl, you've found your man. So this isn't the way you imagined it would be; life's no fairy tale, it's complicated. What are you going to do about it? Sit and whine, or get off your bottom and go for it? Life with Josh had the potential to surpass any dream she'd ever had.

There was no point pretending this wasn't going to be a tough nine months for Josh. Her pregnancy was not something they could ignore, it was bound to be a massive problem for him, and his ambivalence was painfully understandable. But she could help him to be positive about it, she *knew* she could. Don't just stand there bleating like a dummy, Flora, make it work!

'And marrying me would be drastic?'

'Does it get much more drastic?' she asked wryly.

It was a relief to finally come to terms with the conflict that had raged within her. She still felt apprehensive, but now she was fired up and determined. It was time to start doing something positive—something like marrying the man she loved and showing him that the past couldn't hurt them! It would be worth the wait.

Josh was unaware of what she was thinking; his expression had grown darkly sombre. 'How about having a baby? That's the definition of desperately drastic in my book.'

'It's the definition of fulfilling in mine, Josh.' Her face shone with a new serenity.

'Have you seen a doctor yet?'

'Yes.'

'Who is he? I'll check him out...'

'In case he turns out to be an addict?'

Josh winced and his eyes darkened. 'I didn't mean...'

'To interrogate me? I know what you mean to do,' she added quietly. 'You mean you'd like to wrap me up in cotton wool and treat me like an invalid. I knew you'd overreact if I told you... Well, I won't have it, Josh.'

'The way I recall it you thought I'd insist you had an abortion,' he reminded her grimly.

Flora flushed defensively. 'Do you blame me?'

Josh narrowed his eyes and didn't reply immediately. 'Actually I was going to point out that twins run in our family, it's something we ought to mention to your obstetrician.'

Flora's mouth and eyes opened wide simultaneously. *Twins!* She hadn't considered that. *'We...?'* she managed, regaining a little of her composure. 'When you say run, Josh, just how many twi—'

Josh cut her off abruptly. 'I'm not going to be a silent partner, Flora,' he warned her.

She trembled but didn't protest as one of his big hands curled over her flat belly. It was the first time she hadn't felt lost and lonely in a long time.

'You have to promise me if at any stage during this...' he swallowed as though saying the word was hard for him '...*pregnancy* you are at risk in any way you'll put your own well-being first.' His voice firmed as he met her startled gaze sternly. 'Do you understand what I'm saying, Flora?'

She did. If it came to a choice between her and the baby he wanted her to choose herself. How could she promise that, when even though the life within her was hardly formed the same couldn't be said for her new and powerful maternal feelings?

She wanted to hug him and tell him everything was going to be all right, but she knew he wouldn't believe her. 'I understand what you're saying, Josh, and I have to tell you I don't much care for your tone.' She tried with limited success to lighten the atmosphere.

'The word *tough* springs to mind. And just for the record,' he added a shade belligerently, 'I don't much like you not telling me you're carrying my child. Were you going to…?'

'I don't know,' she admitted in a distracted voice. 'Can't you just be optimistic…?' she suggested wistfully. 'Do you always have to be…?'

'Practical! One of us needs to be!' he thundered.

Flora's mind was racing. 'If I marry you will that constitute practical?' It was practical when compared to the alternative. The alternative, a life minus Josh, didn't bear contemplating.

'You mean it?' he grated. Gloatingly triumphant, his glowing eyes moved hungrily over her face. 'You better had!' he warned her grimly.

She lifted her hand and pressed her fingers to his lips. 'Stop,' she pleaded, 'before you demonstrate what a classically macho overbearing husband you'll make. I know I'm probably crazy, but the simple truth is you were right—I'm not sure I can live without you,' she announced with a sob. To hell with pride! 'It seems wicked to say it, but I'm not sure I'd want to live without you.'

When she managed to blink away the tears from her eyes she saw that Josh seemed to appreciate the enormity of her husky confession. In fact he looked so stunned she wasn't sure if she'd scared him off with the intensity of her feelings.

Her doubts only lasted a few seconds before he groaned harshly and lunged towards her, his arms lifting her off the ground as his lips offered hungry, incontrovertible proof of his pleasure.

When he finally drew back Flora found herself standing in the circle of Josh's strong arms with her head on his shoulder, conscious of the soothing background throb of his steady heartbeat. She inhaled deeply, her senses greedily drinking in the unique male fragrance that was just his alone.

'I hope you realise that a kiss like that is equivalent to an engagement ring?'

'A real rock,' she agreed dreamily. 'I knew this would happen if I ever opened my door for you.' She gave a contented sigh and rubbed her cheek against the thin fabric of his shirt, breathing in the smell of the warm musky scent of him. A sharp thrill of sexual desire shot through her. 'You've no idea how hard it was not to when you were hammering on it for what seemed like hours. I thought you'd never go away.'

'That didn't seem like hours, it was hours, and if I'd known for sure you were here I would have put up a stronger resistance when that pair of butch security guys expelled me from the building!'

'I didn't contact them,' she promised, lifting her head. 'It was the neighbours. This is a very respectable building.'

'I feel I know all the neighbours personally—the whole damned building came to watch the floorshow when the heavy mob arrived. Actually the general consensus from those who know me seems to be I'm a pretty respectable type myself these days.'

'Do I detect a tiny note of regret there?' she teased lightly.

'I regret a lot things, Flora,' he admitted with none of the levity her own voice had contained. 'But, believe me, meeting you is not one of them. Believe me too when I say I'll make you the very best husband I know how.' He just hoped to hell that was going to be good enough! Tenderly his fingers trailed down her smooth cheek.

The throb of sincerity in his voice brought an emotional

lump to her throat. She turned her head to kiss the palm
of the hand that caressed her face.

'I believe you, Josh.'

'We've got a lot to plan, there's no point hanging
around. We don't need anything fancy...' He looked ready
to dash off and collar a willing priest right there and then.
If she was going to do the wedding thing, she thought, it
might be quite nice to do it properly—after all she had no
intention of doing it more than once. Right now she had
more urgent things on her mind so she didn't think it necessary to break this to him straight off.

'I think you should get your priorities right from the
start.' Rather boldly she flicked open the top button of his
shirt and made a gentle circular exploratory movement
over his hair-roughened skin with one curious finger. She
lifted her eyelashes to take a sultry little peek at his reaction. It was promising—*very* promising!

'You put forward a very convincing argument,' he admitted throatily.

Flora took him by the hand and led him towards her
bedroom door. She knew for sure that, no matter how
much they had going against them, as long as he continued
to look at her like that they had more going for them!

Flora loved watching Josh work. He attacked a canvas with
bold, sure strokes, yet there was nothing insensitive about
his rich, vibrant style. He liked to paint her and there were
several portraits stacked around the walls that lovingly
showed the many stages of her expanding girth.

The light in this studio Josh had created in their new
home still excited him and Flora approved of things that
made Josh happy. She made Josh happy, but she was also
aware that she and the child growing big within her were
responsible for the growing tension she sensed in him.

It still felt strange being Mrs Prentice, but not unpleasant strange—no, a long *long* way from unpleasant! The reality of being with Josh surpassed her wildest dreams. He'd indulged her when she'd told him she wanted their wedding to be a special day to share with their family and friends, though he'd had a hard time keeping his impatience in check as the preparations were being made.

Flora didn't actually have a lot of family, but the enormous Prentice clan more than compensated. Liam had made a delightful page, and though Flora had thought at first that she'd never be able to look at Jake and his wife without blushing the couple had soon put her at her ease. Nowadays the brothers complained that the two women were constantly conspiring together behind their backs.

Josh tried hard to hide his anxiety from her, but she occasionally—more often lately—caught a fleeting fearful expression in his grey eyes that you could almost taste. It made her ache with bitter-sweet empathy. She knew that until she had safely delivered their child Josh wouldn't be able to throw off the ghosts from the past that haunted him—that haunted their union.

Quietly so as not to disturb him she got up from the canvas studio chair. The combination of the flimsy chair and her bulk made quiet hard to achieve. Josh turned around and she responded before he'd asked.

'I'm fine. I could just do with a stretch.'

She didn't mention the nagging pain in her back because Josh had a habit of overreacting to every trivial ailment, and as often as not she responded crankily in return to his concern, and before you could blink they were arguing. Hormones might be responsible, but Flora found she had lost her appetite for conflict; happily for them both that was the only appetite she'd lost.

'Anyone home?' Alec, Josh's agent, came in through

the garden door bringing a sharp blast of cool air with him. 'I have to come and thank this brilliant husband of yours.'

'I wish you wouldn't feed his ego,' Flora pleaded drolly.

Alec regarded her uncertainly. He could never quite work out when Josh's new wife was joking. 'I sold those shares!' he announced exultantly to Josh who was regarding his canvas with a critical eye.

'What shares would those be?'

'What shares?' Alec shook his head disbelievingly. 'The man says what shares!' he repeated to Flora.

'I heard you the first time, Alec.'

'I've made a small fortune!' his agent enthused. 'I could retire, not that I'm going to,' he added hastily.

'I'm relieved,' Josh responded drily. 'And happy for you.'

'Why,' Flora wondered out loud, 'would you take Josh's advice about shares?'

Alec looked from Flora to Josh. 'She's joking...right? She does know...?'

'Know what? Do you dabble...?' She broke off as Alec broke down laughing like a drain. 'Why do I get the feeling I'm missing something here?' she appealed with growing impatience to her husband.

'When Jake and I were eighteen we inherited some money from our grandmother about the same time we were given a project in school which involved investing—on paper—a given amount of money on the stock exchange to see if we could make a profit.' He shrugged and laid down his brush. 'I did make a profit, only I did it for real with gran's inheritance.'

'That was reckless,' she murmured. But not entirely unexpected, she thought wryly, having come to know her husband's reckless streak. Though he was more the mother hen upon occasion with her than the bold reckless pirate he reminded her of.

'That's what my mother said, amongst other things, when she found out. The outcome of that first foray was that I discovered early on that I had a knack for making a bit of money,' he explained diffidently.

How much? she wondered as she watched Josh frown repressively at his agent, who seemed to find his last off-hand statement incredibly amusing.

'Being a card-carrying member of the financial establishment must have hurt your credibility as the rebel artist with attitude.'

Josh grinned at this side swipe. 'On the plus side it meant I didn't have to dance to the tune of money-grubbing philistines like Alec here—nothing personal, mate.'

'Today, my friend, you can do no wrong,' Alec assured him sunnily.

'You're rich, aren't you…?' Suddenly she understood the fact he hadn't shared her concern about the extortionate price label attached to their lovely new home. He could obviously afford to be blasé. 'I mean *really* rich.'

'It's all relative, but I suppose I am,' he conceded, wiping an oily smear from his hand with a cloth.

Flora's eyebrows arched. 'And it didn't occur to you to mention this before we got married?'

'I was having a hard enough time getting you to the altar as it was,' he reminded her candidly. 'I didn't want to risk you having moral qualms about being hitched to a dirty capitalist. Besides, it doesn't really matter, does it?'

Alec, a very literal soul who had missed all the subtle interplay, began to bear the worried look of a man who was witnessing serious marital discord. 'He gives loads of stuff away, Flora,' he piped up anxiously. 'That new ward at the children's hospice… The research…'

'Shut up, Alec!' Josh snapped.

'Yes, shut up, Alec,' Flora mimicked, her warm glance still resting on her husband's flushed face. 'Can't you see you're embarrassing Joshua?'

Alec gave a relieved sigh. 'She doesn't mind, then.'

'No,' Flora agreed softly, 'she doesn't mind. Besides, like the man said, it doesn't really matter.' Her glowing blue eyes were transmitting an unambiguous message of love as she gazed over at the tall man she'd married. 'We've got our priorities straight,' she explained.

'I love you!' Josh, much to his agent's acute discomfort, breathed fervently.

Flora smiled contentedly as a warm glow enveloped her. 'If you two gentlemen will excuse me…I thought I might have a nap before Liam gets back from Oliver's. What time are the Smiths bringing him back?'

'Don't worry about that, you just rest. I'll deal with Liam.'

Flora stifled a yawn. 'Maybe I'll let you. You know, there are compensations for having a husband who works from home.'

'Even if I am always under your feet?'

She appeared to consider the question. 'On balance,' she conceded grudgingly. 'I think I quite like having you around.'

Josh looked in and found Flora still asleep after he'd bathed Liam later that evening. He decided to put the little boy to bed without disturbing her. Several stories later—he'd resorted to simple and effective bribery when the toddler had taken some convincing he couldn't go and climb into bed with Flora—Josh closed the door quietly on the sleeping cherub.

Anxious not to disturb his wife, he cautiously opened their bedroom door.

'What are you doing?' He looked with a confused frown when he discovered her kneeling on the bedroom floor with her upper body resting on the rumpled bed.

Flora paused in her panting to cast him a withering look; her face was blotchily red and sweaty. 'What does it look like?'

'Oh, God!' Josh went completely still. 'You're not... you can't be!'

'Want to bet...?'

Josh's white, bloodless lips moved, but nothing emerged. The aghast silence lengthened as no coherent words formed in his frozen brain.

The almost feral sound that emerged from Flora's lips jolted him from his catatonic trance.

'Ambulance...' he gasped. 'I'll ring, or shall I drive...?' He thrust his shaking hands into his trouser pockets and hoped that wouldn't be necessary. 'And the Smiths will come over for Liam. Don't go anywhere!'

Flora found a cold spot on the bed cover and pressed her cheek into it as a merciful gap occurred in what seemed to be one long, unremitting contraction. What had happened to slow and gradual...?

'I'm not going anywhere and neither are you...*please*, Josh! I've already called the ambulance, but I'm pretty certain that they won't get here in time.' Being a relative novice at this sort of thing, she might be wrong—only she wasn't taking any chances. If Josh wanted to get out he'd have to step over her to do so.

Josh shook his head. 'That can't be right,' he babbled,

raking a shaky, distracted hand through his dark hair. 'First labours are long, everyone says so...'

'Try telling that to this baby! Oh!' She gasped, turning a pain-distorted face towards him. 'It's started again... *Josh!*' she pleaded, stretching a fluttering hand towards him. 'I don't know what to do.'

At the sight of her pain-racked little face he grabbed his own gut-freezing fears unceremoniously by the scruff and put them firmly to the back of his mind. Flora needed him, and, inadequate though he felt to the task, he was going to help her through this any way he could.

'It's all right, sweetheart,' he crooned, getting down on his knees beside her. He brushed the damp hair from her eyes. 'I'm here.'

The small hand that slid inside his tightened as she turned to rest her head against his chest. 'I woke up,' she said, 'and it was just happening. I rang the ambulance, I didn't want to worry you too soon...'

Josh's expression tightened. 'You can forget about tip-toeing around my feelings, angel, I'm fine. Just think about what you're doing.'

Right at that moment her body was telling her exactly what she had to do and she couldn't have ignored the instructions if she'd wanted to. 'You know how I said I didn't know what to do...?'

Josh nodded.

'I do now! I've got to pushhh...!' She groaned.

Somehow Josh managed to get her back onto the bed. The sweat was pouring down his face, but not from the effort of lifting her.

Although he'd always known what the end result was meant to be, he'd been too caught up in his recurring night-mare, the one when he lost Flora, to be prepared for the emotional and physical impact of the warm slippery body of their new daughter when she landed in his hands.

Tears mingled with the other moisture on his face as he placed the stridently complaining baby on her mother's chest.

'She's absolutely perfect!' he breathed incredulously.

Then all his attention and concern returned anxiously to the new mother who was quietly sobbing. He placed his hands palm flat on either side of her face and moved them very gently, slowly downwards until they came to rest on her slender shoulders as if to convince himself she was still there.

'You're all right!' he breathed wonderingly.

'Better than that,' she replied, tearing her eyes from the small dark-haired bundle in her arms. '*Much* better. You look better too,' she added. The moment was made more perfect because she knew that the last barrier to their happiness had been lifted...she watched him realise it too. Two perfect moments in one day!

'I feel...' He flexed his shoulders and rolled his neck. At a loss to describe the feeling of a planet-sized burden being lifted. 'I want to laugh like an idiot.'

'Go ahead!' she advised jubilantly. 'You did it!' she told him, triumph shining in her teary eyes. 'I *knew* you could.'

'From where I was standing it looked to me like *you* did it.'

'We did it, I knew we could,' she purred complacently. It was amazingly easy to dismiss a fraught few minutes back there when she'd thought she couldn't! Poor Josh, she'd told him so in no uncertain terms.

'We can do anything together! Though next time,' Josh modified, 'I'd prefer not to do this much *everything*...'

'Next time!' she mocked, grinning at the expression of

amazement that spread over his face when he realised what he'd said.

'I didn't mean that's up to…'

'I know what you meant, idiot…what's that?'

'The ambulance crew, I expect.'

'Then you'd better go let them in before they break down the door, or wake Liam.' Hers eyes widened. 'What will he say when he wakes up in the morning and finds he's got a little sister?'

'He won't wake up to find a little sister because his little sister and his mother will be safely tucked up in a hospital bed.' His 'this isn't negotiable' glare stilled the protest on her lips. 'Do this for me, Flora. I want you to have a proper check-over.'

She nodded. It wasn't much of a concession to make when you thought about the enormous one he'd made. 'About her name,' she called out as he went to leave the room. 'I thought Emily for my mother. Emily Bridget has a nice ring, I think… Do you…?' She gave him a tentative half-smile.

Tears glittered in Josh's eyes. 'The day I followed you turned out to be the luckiest day of my life!' he announced authoritatively, his deep voice throbbing with conviction.

'Mine too, baby,' she crooned softly to their daughter. 'You don't know it yet, but you've got the best daddy in the entire world.' And I have the best man, she thought as she sat back to enjoy a brief, blissful moment of quality time with her new daughter.

Getting down to business in the boardroom... and the bedroom!

A secret romance, a forbidden affair, a thrilling attraction...

What happens when two people work together and simply can't help falling in love—no matter how hard they try to resist?

Find out in our new series of stories set against working backgrounds.

Look out for

THE MISTRESS CONTRACT
by Helen Brooks, Harlequin Presents® #2153
Available January 2001

and don't miss

SEDUCED BY THE BOSS
by Sharon Kendrick, Harlequin Presents® #2173
Available April 2001

Available wherever Harlequin books are sold.

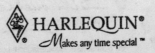

Visit us at www.eHarlequin.com   HP925

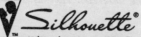

INDULGE IN A QUIET MOMENT
WITH HARLEQUIN

Get a FREE

*Quiet Moments
Bath
Spa*

with just two proofs of purchase from
any of our four special collector's editions in May.

Harlequin® is sure to make your time special this Mother's Day
with four special collector's editions featuring a short story
PLUS a complete novel packaged together in one volume!

Collection #1   Intrigue abounds in a collection featuring *New York Times*
bestselling author Barbara Delinsky and Kelsey Roberts.

Collection #2   Relationships? Weddings? Children? = *New York Times*
bestselling author Debbie Macomber and Tara Taylor Quinn
at their best!

Collection #3   Escape to the past with *New York Times* bestselling author
Heather Graham and Gayle Wilson.

Collection #4   Go West! With *New York Times* bestselling author
Joan Johnston and Vicki Lewis Thompson!

Plus Special Consumer Campaign!
Each of these four collector's editions will feature a
"FREE QUIET MOMENTS BATH SPA" offer.
See inside book in May for details.

Only from
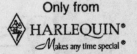
HARLEQUIN®
Makes any time special ®

Don't miss out! Look for this exciting promotion on sale in May 2001,
at your favorite retail outlet.